Just Wild About Harry

Just
Wild
About
Harry

A MELO-MELO IN SEVEN SCENES BY

Henry
Miller

A NEW DIRECTIONS BOOK

Manufactured in the United States of America
First published clothbound (ISBN: 0–8112–0320–4) in 1963 and as
New Directions Paperbook 479 (ISBN: 0–8112–0724–2) in 1979

New Directions Books are published for James Laughlin
by New Directions Publishing Corporation,
80 Eighth Avenue, New York 10011

SECOND PRINTING

Dedicated to Renate Gerhardt

INTRODUCTION

Those who have read *Nexus* (Volume 1) will recall that I devoted some hallucinating pages to a description of my first attempt to write a play, an effort which never got beyond Act One. That was about the year 1926 or '27, since which time I made no further efforts in this direction until two years ago, while staying in the town of Reinbek, Germany. It was there, at the Rowohlt Verlag, that I met Herr Krieschke of the Theatre Department. He was convinced that I could write a play and should. Of course I had toyed with the idea over and over again during the intervening years, but every time I got serious about it my courage failed me. It was not only the remembrance of that first dismal failure which stymied me but the conviction that my natural style of writing was opposed to the dramatic form. It was something of a miracle that I was able to hatch this anomalous "melo-melo" with all its shortcomings.

It came about—*happened* is the word—very much the way I made my first water color. I was lonely, hungry, and had nothing better to do. I sat down that Christmas Eve (1960) and told myself to begin. I hadn't the slighest notion of what I would write. In three days I had finished the first rough draft. It was almost as if it had been dictated to me. About six weeks later I sat down and rewrote it. And that was all there was to it.

If this strikes the reader as incredible, let him read what Ionesco says about his method of work. Here is what he says: "Vous savez, je ne sais jamais raconter mes pièces. . . . Tout est dans les répliques, dans le jeu, dans les images scéniques, c'est très visuel, comme toujours. . . . C'est une image, une première réplique, qui déclenche toujours, chez moi, le mécanisme de la création, ensuite, je me laisse porter par mes propres personnages, je ne sais jamais où je vais exactement. . . . Toute pièce est, pour moi, une aventure, une chasse, une découverte d'un univers qui se révèle à moi-même, de la présence duquel je suis le premier étonné. . . ."[1]

As early as 1913, when first I heard Emma Goldman lecture (in San Diego, California), I became interested in the drama. All through the Twenties I was an ardent theatregoer. For a time during this period my wife June played a number of roles with the Theatre Guild group. In addition to attending plays I read plays, hundreds of them, I should imagine, including some bizarre ones such as *Gammer Gurton's Needle, Brokenbrow* and *Le Cocu Magnifique*. I was particularly fond of the ancient Greek drama and of the Elizabethan playwrights such as Marlowe, Webster and John Ford. Of all the plays I have seen John Ford's *'Tis Pity She's a Whore* moved me most. I saw it for the first and only time in French, at the old Atelier in Montmartre. The Russian dramatists also affected me profoundly, as well as the German Expressionists. I read them all—French, Austrian, Ital-

<hr>

[1] From *En Francais dans le Texte:* "Le Dramaturge malgré lui." By Louis Pauwels, Jacques Mousseau, Jean Feller: Editions France Empire, Paris, 1962.

ian, Spanish, Norwegian, anything and everything I could lay hands on.

The Twenties was a wonderful period in the history of the American theatre, due largely to the liberal importation of foreign plays. Bernard Shaw's name was on everyone's lips then, as well as Eugene O'Neill's. To be followed soon by Sean O'Casey who, in my opinion, is a better dramatist than Shaw ever was. But what a delight—and even a shock—it was to see for the first time a curtain raiser like *Androcles and the Lion*. Or, for that matter, Toller's *Masse Mensch* or Kaiser's *From Morn till Midnight*.

Curiously enough, it was after seeing Saroyan's *Time of Your Life,* which is by no means a great play, that I began to think I might one day do something in this medium myself. It seemed so easy and natural to write as Saroyan did. Besides, I was thoroughly fed up with the social-psychological drama, which Americans still seem to dote on. However, I did nothing. It required a stronger dose than Saroyan to do the trick. This I got when I saw *Waiting for Godot,* in Paris, the opening night. The dose was renewed some time later on seeing Ionesco's *The Chairs* and *The Bald Soprano*.

But to go back a bit . . . My theatregoing began at the age of seven or eight. Every Saturday my mother gave me a dime with which to buy a seat in "nigger heaven" at the Novelty Theatre (a vaudeville house) on Driggs Avenue, Brooklyn (the 14th Ward). I continued this routine, with occasional lapses to attend a bloodcurdling melodrama (such as one could be sure to enjoy at Corse

Payton's Theatre, Brooklyn), or a musical like *Wine, Woman and Song*. Until the day came when I saw my first burlesque show. (I was just seventeen.) From then on, until I went to France, I was a devotee of burlesque. Nothing would please me better, even at this late age, than to write a few comic bits of a genre such as those lovable slapstick comedians of the past exploited to the hilt. Who knows, perhaps that crude mixture of humor and obscenity which abounded in burlesque had much to do with the employment of these elements in my own work. They are two elements, incidentally, which are as old as the theatre itself. And they may be revived one day, when we have freedom of speech once again— or just freedom.

While in France I became acquainted with the writings of Antonin Artaud, especially his views about the theatre. His ideas hit me very much as once did the fiery propaganda of the I.W.W. Here was revolution, genuine revolution. Except for a small circle of admirers, no one seemed to take Artaud's views seriously. *Literature*, that's all it was. Besides, wasn't he a bit of a madman? (What innovator isn't?) People don't want to be hit in the guts; they don't want to go all out; they don't want to revolutionize things day in and day out. As for "revolutionizing oneself every day," as Blaise Cendrars put it, that is still unthinkable. Only saints and gurus have the courage to entertain such ideas.

Naturally, I don't pretend to have done anything revolutionary in writing this play. (Or did I whistle it?) To be frank, I am delighted merely to have succeeded in breaking the ice. Maybe I can do another, and another.

The important thing is that I conquered an old fear, the fear that I was not cut out to write plays. But, as I have frequently remarked, I was not cut out to be a writer either. To write was the last thing on earth left me to attempt; at everything else I had been a rank failure. That I have been able to toss off what passses for books still baffles me. To be sure, I was steeped in books from a very early age. Reading has always been a vice with me, a well-nigh incurable one. In addition I have what some consider the bad habit of identifying myself with the author or his characters. I became the hero of *The Magic Mountain* and behaved like him for quite a time; I even signed my letters "Hans Castorp." Sometimes I took on the personality of Herr Peeperkorn, another character in that work. As for Knut Hamsun, it took me years to slough off the personality of Herr Nagel (in *Mysteries*). I mention just a few. When I think of Dostoievsky I think of a merry-go-round. I lived out so many roles portrayed by his characters (good and bad) that I almost lost my own identity. *Long live the Stavrogins!*

And so, perhaps it is with this play as with my early novels—the unpublished ones. Too many influences, too many voices, too much identification. I have yet to discover the "dramaturge" in myself. Should I worry about it? *March on!* That is my motto. Try again, and again and again. If you can't master it, smash it! Today the revolution is on. And, as Jack London used to say, "it is here to stay." The leaders of the new theatre, I notice, are regarded as being "antitheatre." But what does that mean? Not *against,* as people like to think, but *for.*

For live theatre, theatre freed of its age-old trammels, theatre which enables the spectator to participate and not merely sit back and be entertained or instructed, or even edified. Every vital new movement has for its primary aim to awaken. Wake up and live! Wake up and sing! Wake up and roar like a lion! *Wake up, man!* That is what every creator is shouting through his lines.

With Beckett and Ionesco . . . others too . . . we are witnessing something like an atom-smashing process. What will happen tomorrow no one knows. We are by no means at the end of the road. To build anew one must first tear down the old. And this is now being done with a vengeance.

When we consider the position, the role, the opportunities which are presented to the mathematicians and men of science today it is evident that the artists are being outstripped. The former are not only urged to break new ground but they are handsomely paid to do it. Whereas with the latter all daring is penalized. (Perhaps with good reason, for the artist is even more capable of upsetting the apple cart than the mathematician or the scientist. Once the artist gets the bit between his teeth, good-by this sad, stale world of ours!)

The point I wish to make, however, is this. Antiart is still art. It is not hayseed or wild mustard. It is impossible to kill art; it is part of life itself. No matter how we express ourselves, whatever we do or say with spirit belongs to the world of art. The revolutions which take place in this realm are so many life-breathers. To ask where these revolutionaries are leading us is futile. They are leaders in name only—instruments of the inscrutable life force. "It" knows better than we ourselves. We *think* we know: it *knows*. Naturally it takes time for us to catch on, to discover where we are heading and why. When we wake up the sun is already setting. Once again we find ourselves imprisoned in a mold. And once again, of a bright morning, we wake up and shake ourselves free. That is the way of art and of life.

Henry Miller
July 17, 1962

Just Wild About Harry

This play, if it can be called a play, was inspired by a random remark of Traugott Krieschke's at the Rowohlt Verlag in Reinbek-bei-Hamburg. It was begun in the bedroom of a little boy named Titus, because I had nothing better to do, nowhere to go, and no one to talk to.

TIME: Any old time

PLACE: Any old place

CHARACTERS

HARRY: *Tall, handsome, athletic, rather stuck on himself. In his thirties. Rather awkward—always bumping into things, knocking things over. Has an infectious laugh.*

JEANIE: *Good-looking in a healthy, natural way. Irish type, with long, blonde hair and beautiful eyes. Between twenty-five and thirty. A simple, trusting creature.*

BAR GIRL (*respectable prostitute*): *Her name is never mentioned. About twenty-five but looks much younger. Latin type. Not unintelligent. Has extremely shapely legs and good figure. The type that attracts men.*

DR. KHARKHOVSKI (*pharmacist*): *Small, homely man, rather unpleasant-looking; about fifty. Could be taken for an abortionist.*

YOUNG MAN (*referred to as Romeo*): *About twenty-five. Serious-looking, dark complexion. The poetic type.*

BARMAN (*Louis*): *Middle-aged, foreign-looking; speaks with slight Italian accent.*

HOODLUM: *Typical good-for-nothing. In his early twenties.*

MIDGET: *Undefinable age, typical large head for small body. Sympathetic in tragicomic way.*

POOL PLAYERS and HARRY'S PALS *at table: all nondescript, young, worthless, types. Pool players are thin and cadaverous-looking.*

OTHER CHARACTERS: *Blind man, German street musicians, old messenger, Harry's old mother, house painter (trick cyclist), old hag at the window, big fat German at window, the three drunks, "Mother" (of Mother's Day), four palanquin bearers, two cops, ambulance driver and interne.*

NOTE ABOUT MUSIC

Where possible I have given titles of songs, names of singers or players, name and number of record, for jukebox airs. Do not want substitutes unless good reasons can be advanced. Most of the numbers are given only in snatches; where prolonged, this is indicated in the text. In the last scene the sound should come from high up in the wings.

NOTE ABOUT THE MYNAH BIRD

I recognize the difficulty here, but assume that a good ventriloquist or some such is capable of imitating the Mynah Bird imitating a man's or woman's voice. Thus a tape can be made of the bird's part.

NOTE ABOUT THE CYCLIST HOUSE PAINTER

Naturally he should be a trick cyclist and should probably do a little more business than is actually indicated. If not too corny, he should make a third appearance, this time without smashing into a window. But immediately after he disappears around the corner, there could come the same sound as before—of glass being shattered. Only this time it might have a tinkling sound.

NOTE ABOUT END OF SCENE ONE

If possible, as "Mother" and others exit, the whole façade of houses from left side to intersection of streets should collapse like an accordion, exposing to view (as if accidental) the big bulky German standing with back to audience in his red flannel underwear, swigging his lager beer from a big old-fashioned tin can (the growler) or from a "scuttle of suds."

20

LIST OF MUSICAL NUMBERS REFERRED TO IN
Just Wild about Harry
(given in order of use)

"Ist das nicht ein Gartenhaus, Gartenhaus, Garten-
haus?"
"Silver Threads among the Gold"
"Rumania, Rumania" (as sung by Aaron Lebedeff,
Tenor, Columbia Record No. 8226–7 and No. 29723,
recorded somewhere between 1920 and 1930)
"Sweet Sue—Just You"
"I Can't Give You Anything But Love"
"Moi, mes souliers" (as sung by Felix Leclerc, the com-
poser, Polydor L.P. No. 530,001)
"God Bless America" (as sung by Kate Smith)
"In the Meantime Let Me Tell You That I Love You"
(as sung in the German film *Marina*)
"God Bless America" (as sung by Kate Smith)
"These Foolish Things"
"He's My Man"
"Im Lauterbach hab' ich mein Strumpfer'l verlor'n"
"Two Sleepy People" (Fats Waller Version)
Fifth Piano Sonata of Scriabin
"The Seven Joys of Mary" (as sung by John Jacob Niles)
"Monotonous" (as sung by Eartha Kitt)

"Sweet Sue—Just You"

"I Wonder as I Wander" (as sung by John Jacob Niles)

"Dreamy, Dreamy Chinatown"

"The Musicians" (children's song)

"Row, Row, Row" (from the Ziegfeld Follies of 1914)

"Illusion" (or any other good one of Hildegard Neff's)

"There's No Tomorrow" (as sung by Tony Martin)

"Monotonous" (as sung by Eartha Kitt)

"Old Folks at Home" ("Suwannee River")

"Dancing Cheek to Cheek"

"Ionization" by Edgar Varèse

"I'm Just Wild about Harry!"

"There'll Be a Hot Time in the Old Town Tonight"

"Dancing Cheek to Cheek"

"Hurrah for the German Fifth!" (If unavailable, then use "Harrigan, That's Me"—words and music by George M. Cohan)

"Just a Kiss in the Dark"

"The Stars and Stripes Forever"—John Philip Sousa

"My Wild Irish Rose"

"Introduction and Allegro" by Ravel (as recorded by Grandjany)

"Comin' through the Rye"

Scene One

SCENE ONE

Fantastic street scene in some end-of-the-world part of a city. In broken letters at height of first story is painted "United Nations Street." The narrow houses lean to, fall forward and backward; the walls are crumbling, the doors askew, windows missing. Every other building is a saloon with names like The Velvet Muff, The Dipso's Delight, The Hopheads, Haven for Spastics, etc. The street is broken by three other intersecting streets, named North Second, South Fifth and West Third. Curving through them like a caterpillar runs an Elevated Line. At intervals a gaily painted train (projected on a screen, perhaps) darts through with an awful clatter. In the shop fronts between the saloons are signs reading: "Bidets for sale—cheap!" "Insurance for the Aged" "Corsets, Currycombs and Cobwebs," "Bell Clappers and Binoculars," "Iceboxes to Rent by Day or Week," "Secondhand Rosaries and Crucifixes." The shop windows look meager and pitiful. The Lingerie Shop, for example, has for display one pair of suspenders, one old-fashioned corset, one stringy tie, one silk stocking, one dickey.

From opposite sides enter almost simultaneously the PHARMACIST *and the young* HOODLUM. *They approach lamppost at intersection of streets, surveying one another indifferently. Just as they take up stand at lamppost, a* MIDGET *drags a drunk feet first out of a*

*saloon and ranges the body against a wall of the build-
ing. The* PHARMACIST *(Dr. Kharkhovski) merely shrugs
his shoulders; the* HOODLUM *grins and pulls a cigarette
out of his pocket. He fumbles for a match. The* PHAR-
MACIST *produces a lighter and lights cigarette for him.*
HOODLUM *says nothing, just nods and salutes with two
fingers.*

PHARMACIST Are you expecting someone?

Elevated train darts through. HOODLUM *pretends not
to hear.*

PHARMACIST I say, are you waiting for someone?

HOODLUM Who?

PHARMACIST That's what I'm asking.

HOODLUM *turns his back on the* PHARMACIST *and leans
against lamppost puffing his cigarette. Just as* PHARMA-
CIST *is about to speak again a* HOUSE PAINTER *in white
work clothes enters from left on a bicycle carrying a very
long ladder. He zigzags like a trick cyclist and at intersection of streets, unable to make the turn, smashes a plate-
glass window in one of the shops. He disappears around
the corner to sound of falling glass. Simultaneously with
sound of glass breaking a burglar alarm goes off, and
out of shop comes a little boy playing a harmonica. As he
nonchalantly exits to left, he pauses a moment in front
of a poster reading "Save Your Pennies"[1] and with black
crayon puts a big X over it. The next moment two*

[1] This poster and the others reading "Jesus Saves" and "Fight for
Peace" are printed in repetitive lines which diminish in size as one
reads down. First line can be read from any distance.

Keystone Comedy COPS *appear, clubs in hand. They dash about crazily, as if looking for the culprit, then draw their revolvers and shoot wildly into the smashed window of shop front. That done, they approach the two figures at lamppost.*

FIRST COP (*in squeaky voice to hoodlum*) What are you doing here? What's your business?

HOODLUM Don't ask personal questions.

COP *turns his back, goes to drunk lying against wall, prods him with foot, taps drunk's foot with his club.*

SECOND COP (*to* PHARMACIST) And *you* . . . your name and address!

PHARMACIST Dr. Kharkhovski, pharmacist, of 10396 Whittier Boulevard, Santa Ana.

COP (*seizing him*) You're under arrest.

DR. K. For what?

COP For loitering.

DR. K. Have you a warrant for my arrest?

COP No. (*Starts looking in his pocket.*) Wait a minute. . . .

DR. K. I stand on my rights.

COP What rights?

DR. K. An American cit—

Rest of speech drowned by noise from triphammer in street around the corner.

As the triphammer ceases, the MIDGET *is seen again rolling out a full ash can. He does it so carelessly that the barrel slips from his grasp and the ashes spill out over the stage and the can rolls to the footlights. With this the two* COPS *blow their whistles furiously and dash inside a saloon where there is the sound of men brawling.*

DR. KHARKHOVSKI *is just about to address the* HOODLUM *when a* MESSENGER *in uniform appears bearing a telegram. He is very, very old, totters as he walks, has long white beard like Santa and dark glasses. He is dressed in a gaudy, much braided, tattered uniform much too big for him. He carries a flashlight, and as he approaches the two figures he flashes the light on the wall to read street name.*

HOODLUM (*beckoning with forefinger*) Hey! Whadda ya want?

MESSENGER (*wheezing*) I'm looking for United Nations Street.

HOODLUM (*grabbing telegram*) There ain't no such street. That's for *me*. (*Tears envelope open.*)

MESSENGER Are you Mister Whitcombe Hazlitt of Montebello?

HOODLUM (*reading telegram*) So's your ole man. (*To* DR. K.) He'll be here in a minute now.

MESSENGER (*holding open huge ledger fastened to big belt*) Sign here, please.

HOODLUM (*tearing page out of book, crumpling it*

28

and tossing it away) Scram! (MESSENGER *turns to go without a word.*) Hey! Come back here! Next time make it snappy, hear me? You were three and a half minutes late.

MESSENGER *toddles off mumbling to himself.*

HOODLUM Guess how—

Train darts through with great clatter, drowning his words.

DR. K. Yes?

HOODLUM Guess how old he is!

DR. K. Why should I?

HOODLUM Ninety-two come April. He'll be gettin' a pension soon.

BLIND MAN (*tin cup in hand, enters from left, crying feebly*): Help the blind! Please help the blind!

HOODLUM (*flipping cigarette butt in* BLIND MAN's *direction*) Don't believe a word of it. He's a fake.

Enter from opposite side, crossing BLIND MAN *who is exiting, a rosy-cheeked, dapper-looking* DUDE *in a cutaway, Ascot tie, top hat, gloves, spats, cane, a carnation in his button hole. He walks slowly, like a boulevardier, from one side of stage to other. Before he reaches center of stage* KHARKHOVSKI *speaks.*

DR. K. And *he* . . . who is he, may I ask?

HOODLUM He's a mistake.

As DUDE *reaches center of stage a window above is thrown open and an* OLD WOMAN *dumps a pail of slops out, just barely missing him. And now the* PAINTER *with bike and ladder enters from opposite side, does same tricks as before, and as he rounds corner, smashes another big plate-glass window.*

HOODLUM (*regarding performance stolidly*) Begins to jell, what!

DR. K. Couldn't we stand somewhere else?

HOODLUM No.

DR. K. Why not?

The MIDGET *reappears dragging another drunk out of another saloon—feet first, as before. With this is heard the clanging of an ambulance.* DR. K. *throws up his hands, as if to say—What next? Ambulance, a wreck of an ambulance, makes appearance in the wings.* DRIVER *and* INTERNE *hop out with a stretcher and dash inside building. They reappear in a moment bearing on stretcher a French poodle with one paw bandaged. As they hoist stretcher into ambulance they speak to the poodle in caressing tones.*

DRIVER Sois sage, mon p'tit.

INTERNE Comme tu es beau, mon toutou.

DRIVER Tout ira bien, tu verras.

INTERNE Mon chou. Je t' adore.

While DR. K. *and* HOODLUM *look at one another with an air of disgust the train darts through again.*

DR. K. (*stopping his ears*) What did you say?

HOODLUM I didn't say nuth—

Words drowned by sound of triphammer in street around the corner.
Meanwhile, a window above opens noiselessly and someone unfurls the Cuban flag. HOODLUM *hasn't noticed it.*

DR. K. What's *that* for? (*He points, but* HOODLUM *is looking the other way.*)

HOODLUM Who?

DR. K. What are we waiting for?

Another window opens above and a huge tipsy GERMAN *with handle-bar mustaches leans out and starts singing*: "Ist das nicht ein Gartenhaus, Gartenhaus, Gartenhaus?"

HOODLUM (*jeeringly*) Ja, das ist ein Gartenhaus, Gartenhaus. . . .

GERMAN (*shaking his fist at* HOODLUM) Gott verdammte Hund! (*Slams window down and disappears from sight.*)

HARRY *now appears from round a corner, breathless from running. Waves to the two.* "Hi there!" *As he approaches them, the* MIDGET *reappears from still another building, rolling out a garbage can. He spills it accidentally. Muck scatters in all directions. Can rolls with clatter to footlights.*

HARRY (*kicking the muck away good-naturedly*) What's going on here anyway?

HOODLUM It's Mother's Day.

HARRY (*giving* HOODLUM *a playful push*) You don't say! Since when? (*Pauses a moment to survey* DR. K.) Who's this egg?

HOODLUM Dr. Slivovitz from Belladonna. The guy you're waitin' to see.

DR. K. (*with imperceptible bow*) Dr. Kharkhovski of Santa Ana, California. Pharmacist.

HARRY That's different. (*Extends a paw and shakes* K.'s *hand vigorously.*) Did ya bring yer kit?

DR. K. (*somewhat taken aback*) I think, don't you, that we should discuss this— (*He looks around uneasily.*) Couldn't we find a . . . ?

HARRY (*kicking the muck away*) We can talk right here. There's nuthin' much to yap about anyway. I told you what I wanted.

The HOODLUM *meanwhile, as if totally disinterested, walks up and down, hands in pockets, whistling softly. After a few turns he takes out a big carbide pencil, goes over to poster reading "Jesus Saves" and puts a big X over it.*

DR. K. You were talking to my assistant, Dr. Warschawski, not me.

HARRY Whoever it was, I laid it out plain. (*Slight*

pause) Why the hell don't you answer the phone yourself?

DR. K. It's not quite as simple as you seem to think, Mister . . .

HARRY *Harry*. Just Harry. Don't get nosey, see! (*Suddenly he grabs* DR. K. *by the shoulders, as if to shake him up.*) Whadda ya after . . . more dough? There ain't any more, see! C'mon, man, speak up! I can't stand here all day. (*Turns to call to* HOODLUM.) Hey, call Louis, will yer? Tell him I'll be a little late.

DR. K. Excuse me, Mister . . . I mean *Harry*. This is a very serious matter, you know.

HARRY You're telling *me!*

DR. K. One doesn't take a hammer and chisel and open a . . .

HARRY (*irritated*) Who said anything about a hammer?

DR. K. (*mildly*) That's merely a way of speaking.

HARRY Talk plain. I told you I wanted a nice clean job. No complications.

DR. K. I understand you perfectly, Mister . . . Mister Harry. But we don't rush into these things with two feet, you must understand. One has to approach these matters with a certain amount of caution and circumspection. As I always—

HARRY (*interrupting*) Whatsa matter? Gettin' cold feet already?

DR. K. (*imperturbably*) What I always say is: "Better a baby than a bad conscience. If you really love her, there's always another way out.

HARRY I told you not to rub your nose . . .

DR. K. I don't mean to pry into . . .

HARRY Ya better not!

DR. K. But it's my duty as a physician to warn you that there are two lives at stake.

HARRY Whadda ya gabbin' about? She's only two months . . .

DR. K. In the eyes of the law two months or nine months makes no difference. I only accept these tasks when people are truly desperate.

HARRY The hell you say.

DR. K. (*ignoring the remark*) If for any reason the parents are unable to take care of a child; if one of the parties is insane or feeble-minded; if there are too many children in the family already; if the husband is serving a life sentence, or if he or his wife is hopelessly addicted to drugs, or if . . .

HARRY Or if he can't pay, you mean.

Suddenly an OLD HAG *appears at one of the windows above, screaming* "Help! Murder! Police!"

HARRY Don't mind her. Her ole man's beatin' her up, that's all.

DR. K. I thought it was something serious. As I was saying a moment ago . . .

A cannon cracker goes off round the corner. DR. K. *jumps.*

DR. K. What's that?

HARRY Nuthin'. Just celebratin'.

DR. K. Celebrating what?
More screams from OLD HAG *behind window.*

HARRY Didn't ya hear? *Mother's Day.*

DR. K. As I was saying, Mister Harry . . .

HARRY *now takes up a position, as* DR. K. *begins a long speech, with hands on hips, ears cocked, as if giving the man serious attention. Now and then he nods head gravely, as if concurring, sometimes mumbling Uh-huh, now and then cupping ear or bending head still closer, as if wishing to extract the last drop of meaning from* DR. K.'s *words.*

DR. K. As I was saying (*he gives professional cough*) there's always an element of risk. Post-prandial operandus fecit, we call it. The epithalamium, being unusually sensitive in the infra-uterine region of the pelvis, exposes the subject to aseptic infiltrations alternating with excessive hemorrhages induced by failure of the haemoglobin to respond with its customary elasticity. What's more, the cervical coccyx, when dilated or expanded to interstitial proportions, brings about an eleemosynary condition of the respiratory pustules situated just above the metatarsal sphincter. That is to say, adjacent or contiguous to the ophthalmic urethra. All of which, I need scarcely inform you, is liable to entrain severe hepapatic symptoms of an atrabilious nature. Without due preliminary prognosis, and particularly in view of anticipatory prolapsus provoked by immoderate usage of prophylactic substitutes, certain interpolatory media obfuscated by inflammatory capillaries offer unsuspected proclivities nefarious to the epigastric protoplasm which in turn create serious histological problems. Solutions to these histological problems are always, euphemistically speaking, dangerous—if not downright fatal. On the other hand, the Fallopian viscera when adroitly auscultated have been known to throw off sebaceous matter of peristaltic origin, as evidenced by contumacious research in the field of cybernetics, thus obviating cirrhosis, gangrene, ankylosis and contributary symbiotics. Of course, there remain duodenal factors such as hereditary trauma, somnambulism, inflation of the cornea and other malodorants which occasionally result in an antinomian, sometimes referred to as malignant, excitation of the endocrine ducts, which prior to the introduction of streptococcic remediants were often treated by phlebotomists as symptomatic or consanguineal ulcers. The irruption of mongoloid tissue, morphologically frequent in cases where the oblongata has been damaged, is now successfully combated, particularly in the lumbar and mastoid areas, by subcutaneous irrigation of the lepidoptera or, in pharmaceutical parlance, elytra cornucopia. (*Slight pause*) What I am trying to tell you, Mister Harry, is that the operation, if properly conducted, should be a success—unless the patient succumbs. You follow me?

HARRY (*blinking his eyes*) Of course, of course. Clear as mud.

DR. K. As I remarked before, one has to approach these matters with caution and circumspection. You are aware, I take it, that it may mean twenty years in prison if . . .

HARRY Yeah, I know all that about the clink. That's *my* worry, not yours.

DR. K. We have to be certain, moreover, that the patient is in the proper physical condition to undergo . . .

HARRY You don't need to know nuthin'. I told ya she's O.K. She's young and healthy, and she knows what she's doin'. Ain't that enough?

DR. K. She's over twenty-one, I hope?

HARRY Whadda ya take me fer—a cradle-snatcher? (*Grabs* DR. K.'s *lapels with two hands and pulls him close.*) Listen, you fathead, let's get down to brass tacks. You know what's the matter with you? You've got loggamundiddy of the googoo. (*With this he takes hold of* DR. K.'s *fedora with both hands and pulls it down over his eyes and ears.*) Now tell me what time it is by the hepsidipsera!

He starts dragging DR. K. *toward the wings, right. From the other wing we hear a woman's voice singing* "Darling, I am growing older . . ." (*"Silver Threads among the Gold"*). HARRY *stops in his tracks, turns* round, still clutching DR. K. by the coat sleeve. At same time the MIDGET reappears dragging another drunk out of another saloon feet first. Then he takes the two drunks against the wall and drags them closer to footlights; all three lie at intervals, feet to audience, like railroad ties. Woman is still singing from wings.

From left side "MOTHER" now appears born on a palanquin (reading "Bijou") by four tall, thin, cadaverous-looking undertakers in frock coats, plug hats, black gloves, all with mustaches and goatees. "MOTHER" is a fat, coarse, dowdy-looking creature, grotesquely overdressed, full of paste jewelry, cheeks heavily rouged, eyes heavily made up with mascara and a brilliant, poisonous green over the lids; the eyelashes are very long and her tiny mouth looks like a Cupid's bow. She keeps singing as the palanquin solemnly moves across the stage, but in a tremulous, cracked voice definitely off key. The undertakers step gingerly over the bodies of the drunks and "MOTHER" throws roses to audience from a huge bouquet she carries. As the procession moves along, the sound of the triphammer is heard, but briefly, and the train darts through again with a clatter. Also, one of the saloon doors falls off its hinge with a bang. The MIDGET reappears with another full can, but pauses on threshold of the saloon and watches the procession. As "MOTHER" nears HARRY, he makes the sign of the cross, removes DR. K.'s hat from his head and crushes it underfoot. Just as the palanquin is disappearing, an upper window is violently thrown open and the GERMAN, clad now in red flannel underwear, stands at window and declaims sententiously and in a stentorian voice:

"Jetzt müsste die Welt versinken,
Jetzt müsste ein Wunder gescheh'n!"

HARRY *picks* DR. K.'s *hat up, throws it down furiously,
stamps on it with two feet, and raising his fist to the
German, shouts* "Aw, go fuck a duck!"

CURTAIN

Scene Two

SCENE TWO

Kitchen lighted by shaded bulb suspended from ceiling. Table littered with remnants of food and empty bottles. Sink stacked with dirty dishes. Telephone box hangs on wall opposite sink. A big calendar beside the phone.

As curtain rises, JEANIE, *clad in pajamas and worn bathrobe, hair down and disheveled, is seated at table, back to audience, head in hands, elbows on table. Rises slowly, wearily, her face showing evidence of weeping, and goes to sink, over which there is a large, cracked mirror. As she reaches for the toothbrush she looks at herself in the mirror, nodding her head in disgust and despair. As she is about to brush her teeth the phone rings. She grabs a dirty towel absent-mindedly, starts toward phone, stops, reflects, goes back to sink. Puts toothpaste on brush, bends head down over sink. Phone rings insistently. She drops brush and goes to phone. Picks up receiver and in a hollow voice, as if more dead than alive, says*

JEANIE Yes?

VOICE . . .

JEANIE Yes, it's me.

VOICE . . .

JEANIE No, I'm alright.

VOICE . . .

JEANIE Nothing. I just got up a minute ago.

VOICE . . .

JEANIE I know it. What's the difference?

VOICE . . .

JEANIE (*pausing a moment*) No, he hasn't.

VOICE . . .

JEANIE I don't know. I don't care.

VOICE . . .

JEANIE Maybe he will and maybe he won't.

VOICE . . .

JEANIE Don't worry. I can take care of myself.

VOICE . . .

JEANIE No, please don't. I'd rather be alone.

VOICE . . .

JEANIE I'll try.

VOICE . . .

JEANIE I promise, yes.

The door opens and the MIDGET *stands at the threshold. He pauses a moment, then goes up to* JEANIE, *who hasn't observed his entrance, and tugs her skirt. She turns, looks down at him and smiles.*

VOICE . . .

44

JEANIE Yes, yes. 'Bye now. Someone just came. (*Is about to hang up.*)

VOICE . . .

JEANIE No, not *him*. (*Hangs up.*)

JEANIE *bends down and pinches* MIDGET's *cheeks.*

JEANIE (*a little more animation in voice*) So it's *you!*

MIDGET Such a lovely day. I've been up since dawn. (*Pause*) If it were snowing I would have gone sleigh-riding.

JEANIE (*bending over to kiss his cheek*) You lovely little man! So cheerful, aren't you?

MIDGET (*clapping hands noiselessly*) Yes, aren't I? Always merry and bright, what! I say, is the coffee ready?

JEANIE (*going to refrigerator*) No, but it will be in a minute. (*Extracts bottle of beer.*) Will you have one with me while the coffee boils?

MIDGET You mean while the lentils boil.

JEANIE *puts coffee up, gets rolls from pantry and puts them in the oven, looks for clean dishes.* MIDGET *meanwhile starts to clear the table.*

JEANIE Don't you do a thing. That's *my* job. (*Puts two hands to head.*) God, what a head!

MIDGET (*going to refrigerator and getting out butter, milk, etc.*) It must be about 36 Fahrenheit today. (*Pause*) You don't look too chipper either.

JEANIE (*cheering up a bit*) You're always thinking about the weather, aren't you?

MIDGET (*picking crumb from table and placing it on his tongue*) That's because I haven't much else to think about.

JEANIE (*still busying self with breakfast*). That's what you pretend. I'm sure there's a lot goes on in that little head of yours.

MIDGET It's not so little, you know. Yes, I think once in a while. But I don't get anywhere. Do you?

JEANIE I gave up thinking long ago.

MIDGET Thinking never does any harm, you know. (*Picks up another crumb—*JEANIE *doesn't notice.*) It's worrying that does.

JEANIE (*quaffing her beer*) Or caring too much.

MIDGET Especially for the wrong one. (*Picks up another crumb and puts it in his mouth.* JEANIE *sees this time.*)

JEANIE You're hungry, aren't you? I'm sorry. In a minute now. I have some lovely blackberry jam for you today.

MIDGET (*licking his chops*) Yum yum. It's better than raspberry, isn't it? Especially after a walk.

JEANIE (*motioning for him to sit down*) For a mite of a man you're quite an eater. Always hungry, aren't you?

MIDGET True. But not for bread alone.

JEANIE (*serving coffee and rolls*) Now what does *that* mean?

MIDGET (*deliberately buttering roll, spreading jam, taking good bite, swallowing coffee*) I'll tell you some other time, *maybe*. I'm shy, you know.

JEANIE I know. And I shouldn't be asking so many questions.

MIDGET It's all right to ask, but I don't have to answer. Not if I don't feel like it. Ask me tomorrow—or the day after.

JEANIE Excuse me . . . just one more question.

MIDGET Fire away! (*Stuffs mouth with food, swallows coffee.*)

JEANIE Have you found a job yet?

MIDGET (*smacking his lips*) Yum yum. This jam *is* wonderful. Did you make it yourself?

JEANIE You didn't, did you?

MIDGET (*lowering head, bashful like*) I could use another two bits, if you can spare it.

JEANIE You can have anything you like. Why not two bucks? (*She's eating with seeming relish herself now.*)

MIDGET I don't want that much. It's only till tomorrow. Tomorrow's my lucky day. (*Pause*) You haven't heard anything yet?

JEANIE (*ignoring the question*) Another roll? (*Offers one.*)

47

MIDGET (*takes roll*) I know it's painful. (*He picks up a crumb and places it on his tongue.*) But something's got to be done.

JEANIE Please, let's not talk about it now. I don't want to think about him any more. I'm . . .

MIDGET True. But you can't stop thinking about him, can you?

He continues to eat and drink with gusto, as if only mildly concerned.

JEANIE In this case thinking does no good.

MIDGET (*lightly*) Maybe you're not thinking right.

JEANIE (*about to take a bite, puts it down*) Oh?

MIDGET If I were in love and it was hopeless . . . (*Checks himself.*) Shucks! It's always hopeless, isn't it? All we can do is love.

JEANIE (*bending over table and pinching his two cheeks*) You lovely little man, you. If I were in love with you I'd eat you up.

MIDGET That's my trouble.

JEANIE That you're so lovable?

MIDGET That they want to eat me up. I could be a lump of sugar for all it matters.

JEANIE Don't talk like that. Everyone adores you, you know that.

MIDGET But nobody loves me. Maybe they would if . . .

JEANIE If what? No, I'm sorry. Forget it.

MIDGET *gets up and does a somersault. Resumes place at table and picks up a crumb, but doesn't put it in his mouth this time.*

MIDGET That was easy, wasn't it? I can do other things too. But nobody takes notice. All they see is . . .

JEANIE Maybe it's better so. You'll never lose your heart over a worthless fool.

MIDGET (*excitedly*) Oh no? Shows how much you know. I've got a heart . . . a very big heart too. It could break, if I let it. (*He looks at her in a meaningful way.*) Everyone has a heart to lose. Even chickens. I had a bird once that died of a broken heart. Would you like to hear how it happened?

JEANIE No, not now, please.

MIDGET But it's very interesting. I would even say— instructive.

JEANIE (*rising to get more coffee from stove*) I believe you.

MIDGET Anyway, it's never as terrible as you imagine. Hearts were meant to be broken—like dishes. (*He takes saucer and drops it on floor. It falls to pieces.* JEANIE *looks round in surprise, but says nothing.*)

MIDGET That wasn't him on the phone, was it? He has a heart too, you know. Maybe not so big, but it's a good heart. He never once said a mean word to me. And he's good to children—and animals. Sometimes he says things he doesn't mean, of course.

49

JEANIE You said something there.

MIDGET Men are like that. Women too, sometimes. It's human.

JEANIE It's human to love.

MIDGET And to lie and betray and forget . . . and to make the same mistake a thousand times. You never know what they're up to.

JEANIE But you're not like that.

MIDGET How would *you* know? I never get a chance to show what I'm like. I *can't* do any harm—because nobody takes notice of me.

JEANIE But you wouldn't want to hurt people, would you?

MIDGET (*pausing a moment, a curious expression on his face*) I'm not so sure. It might be interesting.

JEANIE You hurt easy, don't you?

MIDGET It all depends. (*Lowers head slightly.*) *You* could hurt me. (*Looks at her again in meaningful way.*)

JEANIE But I wouldn't want to, would I?

MIDGET It has nothing to do with wanting. (*Pause*) But you can't hurt *him*. Impossible! He's immune.

JEANIE That doesn't mean he can't love, does it?

MIDGET Depends on what you call love. Men are different. Women too, sometimes.

JEANIE I don't understand.

50

MIDGET Of course you don't. You're too . . . You're innocent, that's what.

JEANIE You mean simple.

MIDGET No, I don't. I can explain everything—except innocence.

JEANIE (*leaning toward him, earnestly*) Tell me honestly, do you think I'll ever see him again?

MIDGET (*extracts cigarette from pocket, lights it deliberately*) It's all up to you. You've got to think right. It's not easy either. You must care and not care—at the same time. There's a reason for his acting this way, but he doesn't know it. Neither do we. Some people never come to their senses. With human beings you never know what to expect. Sometimes it's better to expect the worst. (*Pause*) If we were animals, it would be different. Or birds. (*Pause*) The funny thing is, Harry is almost like an animal. I mean in a good way. *Almost,* I say. He never means to hurt anyone. Unless they get in his way. But he's not mean or selfish, that I'm sure of. Forgetful, maybe. (*Slight pause*) He was hurt bad sometime or other. . . .

JEANIE And that makes him hurt *me?*

MIDGET I wouldn't say that. I don't think he knows. . . .

JEANIE (*almost tearfully*) God, if he'd only come back! I love him so much, so much. I'd do anything he asked. *Anything.* I'd crawl on my knees to him, if I thought it would . . .

51

MIDGET (*excitedly*) No, no! Never do that! You'd only scare him away. Better to die of a broken heart.

JEANIE But my heart *is* broken, can't you see?

MIDGET (*shaking his head*) Once it's broken, you're immune.

JEANIE Immune, immune . . .

MIDGET I mean you'll be able to laugh, sing, dance, and nobody'll be the wiser. You'll be like everyone else, only you'll never be able to fall in love again. And so you'll never be hurt again. (*Pauses. Laughs as if to himself.*) I should know. I was born with a broken heart. That's why I make people laugh so easily. (*Another short laugh*) Do you know what the biggest joke is? To fall in love with someone who doesn't even see you. Like you were a worm or a toad. (*Mockingly*) Of course I never do! That would be giving the game away. (*He looks at her again in a meaningful way.*) We don't get much chance to talk about love, people like us. But now and then it happens. We're human too, you know. Maybe too human. You sit here night after night and cry your heart out. We don't do that. We did all our weeping in the womb. (*Pause. Looks at her strangely.*) Supposing I were to burst into tears . . . right now? What would you do? You'd pet me like a dog, wouldn't you? We don't like to be petted that way. (*Pause*) I feel sorry for you. I feel sorry for Harry too. I can't feel sorry for myself, because I haven't even got a chance. (*He starts going toward the door.*) Don't forget the two bits. (*Holds out his hand.* JEANIE *turns her back to get purse*

52

from drawer. He makes a wry grimace.) And supposing your heart is broken—it's better than dying of cancer, isn't it? (JEANIE *puts money in his extended hand. Smiles apologetically.*) If I run into Harry I'll tell him you found someone else. Then he'll come running. (*His hand is on the door knob.*) That's how men are. And women too, godddam it all!

JEANIE (*rushing to him and putting hand on his shoulder*) Forgive me for heaping my troubles on you. You're such a very dear man. (*Impulsively*) I love you very much.

MIDGET (*bowing slightly, half earnest, half in jest*) Thank you, thank you. (*Smiles mysteriously.*) If only you hadn't added—*very much!* (*Then, merrily*) Ta ta! See you tomorrow. (*Exits.*)

JEANIE *closes door after him and locks it. Goes back to the table, puts her head in her hands, and weeps silently. After a few moments she raises her head, and with a look of deep anguish, begins to speak.*

JEANIE It can't go on forever. Something's *got* to happen. If only he'd walk in . . . *now.* Where can he be? Not a word. Not even a little note. It's cruel, cruel. (*She gets up and paces slowly back and forth.*) And why, why? What did I ever do? Love him too much? (*Puts her two hands to face; her shoulders convulse.*) I give up. I can't figure it out. *I love him*—that's all I know. And I'll never stop loving him. (*Pause, reflective*) I know you're not mean, Harry. I know you've got a good heart. But to leave me in the dark, to walk off without

53

a word . . . I don't understand. I wouldn't care what you did—if only you'd tell me. (*Goes to table, sits down again. Flops down, rather, as if utterly exhausted.*) I'll go nuts, nuts. There *must* be some solution. (*Pause*) *Think right.* Isn't it right to want him back? That's all I can think. Dear God, is that too much to ask? What *should* I pray for then? *Is there a God,* I wonder? Maybe I'm not thinking right. I'm *so* mixed up. Help me, somebody! Help me to think straight! (*She stops abruptly, jerks herself upright, a look of determination in her face. Reaches for glass which is almost empty. Drains it. Bangs the glass down, as if that were the last drop she'd ever take.*) I know what I'll do. I'll go and look for him. I'll go to the ends of the earth, if I have to. I'll crawl. What difference does it make? I'm nothing any more . . . *nothing.* (*She goes to telephone and looks up a number in the book.*) It's just possible he's there. (*Starts pacing back and forth, undecided whether to phone or not.*) Should I or shouldn't I? (*Goes to refrigerator to get another bottle of beer. Puts hand on bottle, shoves it back, slams refrigerator shut.*) Maybe I ought to just walk in on him. (*Shakes her head.*) No, he wouldn't like that. (*Paces slowly, head down, chin in hand.*) I'll phone. At least I'll know if he's there or not. Jesus, he could be in California for all I know. Or dead. . . .

Slowly, deliberately, she moves to the phone and lifts the receiver.

CURTAIN

54

Scene Three

SCENE THREE

A cosy, intimate, run-down joint, not too well lighted: combination bar and poolroom. Table up front with bird cage to one side. In it a mynah bird, only partly visible. To right of table, at a little distance, a jukebox. To the rear a pool table. On the wall a rack with cues. At end of bar, only partially visible, a telephone booth.

As curtain rises music (Rumania, Rumania—in Yiddish) is heard quite strongly. The BARMAN *is wiping the bar, cleaning glasses, stacking them. One of the pool players is stacking cues in the rack; another is seated on a low chair, head in hand, nodding, as if snatching a little sleep. The third pool player is stretched out on the pool table, cue in hand, hat over his eyes, apparently sound asleep. At the table up front the* HOODLUM *and two pals are seated, languidly interested in business in hand. One is making boats with paper napkins; the other is whittling at something under the table with a Boy Scout knife; the* HOODLUM *is trying to build a skyscraper with matchboxes. They continue this nonsense throughout the scene. They also get up frequently to go to the bar, to the phone, to play the jukebox, and so on. The pool players, more dead than alive, move about like ghosts, with no talk between them while playing. The sound of balls clicking is heard intermittently throughout scene.*

The record stops and there is a momentary silence.

Then, to the strains of "Sweet Sue," HARRY enters. He's full of pep, bouncy, jovial and boisterous. As he greets his pals at the table the MYNAH BIRD says: "Look who's here!" HARRY *stands a moment, looking the joint over, then waves to the BARMAN. Suddenly he notices the guy asleep on the pool table. He goes to the table, pulls the sleeper toward him by the two legs, and shoves him off. Then he goes to the rack for a cue.*

HARRY (*to the player near rack*) Stack 'em up!

Man does so while HARRY chalks his cue.

HARRY Watch this! (*He takes a slow, steady aim, like a professional, and shoots. Cue slips and makes a rent in the cloth.*)

PLAYER ON CHAIR (*sleepily*) Now look what you went and done!

HARRY *takes torn end of cloth and rips it back clear to the other end, then throws it behind him on the floor. Goes to the rack and selects another cue. Chalks it carefully. Aims again.*

HARRY Now watch!

He makes a bad shot. Throws cue on table in disgust. Picks it up again, places it over his knee and breaks it in two. Drops the two pieces on the table, turns and goes to the table up front. One of the players languidly picks the torn cloth from the floor and puts it back in position. He starts playing, as if nothing had happened. The others take turns shooting. After every shot they cough, wheeze, double up. They move about slowly, like ele-

58

phants. As HARRY *takes seat at table the* HOODLUM *rises and goes to the jukebox.* HARRY *is talking excitedly to the others, but is only half audible. Laughs and slaps his thigh. Music plays—"I Can't Give You Anything But Love."*

HARRY (*audibly*) . . . always asking if I loved her. *Love me still?* Sure I do. *Do what?* Love you. *How much?* Enough to drive yuh nuts. (*Beckons to* BARMAN.) Whatta we havin'? (*Puts up four fingers. Takes a look around. Makes grimace—music too loud. To* HOODLUM) Tone it down, for Chrissake!

HOODLUM *gets up—face always expressionless—goes to jukebox, fools around with it.* HARRY *starts talking again, but is only half audible. Music plays "Moi, mes souliers."*

HARRY (*turning his head to listen better*) What's *that?* What's he singing? (HOODLUM, *moving back to table, shrugs his shoulders.*)

THE WHITTLER (*without looking up*) Hungarian probably.

HARRY It's gettin' more and more like a morgue here. (*Moves head and shoulders to rhythm of music.*) Kinda good, what?

The one with the matchboxes struggles to make sky-scraper, almost succeeds. Then they tumble. HARRY *with sweep of arm gathers boxes to his side.*

HARRY (*always showing off*) Here, let *me* show ya!

Starts building, doesn't get far, fails. He sweeps the

59

boxes onto the floor with one swipe of arm. HOODLUM *rises and gathers them up—without a word or gesture of annoyance.*

BARMAN *now serves beer all around.* HARRY *raises his glass immediately and drinks. The others, seemingly too interested in business in hand, leave theirs untouched.*

MYNAH BIRD (*real comical*) Say, that's real beer!

The one making paper boats gets up and starts toward bar. HARRY *grabs his arm and spins him around.*

HARRY Where yuh goin'? Whattsa matter, can't ya sit still a sec?

THE ONE If you wanna know, I'm gonna take a leak.

HARRY Okay. But make it snappy. And get yourself a new bladder sometime!

The sound of balls clicking. Suddenly one drops into a pocket with a thud.

HARRY Whadda ya know—*he made it!*

HOODLUM *rises, starts toward jukebox.*

HARRY Where *you* goin'? Can't ya sit still?

Ignoring him, HOODLUM *goes straight to jukebox, gives it a shake, drops a coin. Sound of jiggers moving. Suddenly music gives with a blast—Kate Smith singing "God Bless America!"* HARRY *jumps to his feet.*

HARRY (*really angry; to* HOODLUM) Choke it, you louse, you!

HOODLUM *shuts it off obediently, without expression. There is a momentary silence.*

HARRY (*to the one whittling away, head down*) Hey you! Don't you have to go somewhere?

Guy automatically rises and heads for the phone booth.

HARRY (*to himself*) A sociable lot. (*Beckons to* BAR-MAN.) Hey, Louis! (*to himself again*) I shoulda brought ma knittin'. (*To* BARMAN) A deck of cards!

MYNAH BIRD Easy does it.

HARRY (*irritated, looking in bird's direction*) One of these days I'll wring your bloody neck!

MYNAH BIRD You're full of beans!

The three cronies now file back one by one and resume places at the table. Each goes back to his little business. Sound of balls clicking.

THE ONE WITH PAPER BOATS (*not looking up*) What's on your mind, Big Boy?

HARRY Plenty.

BARMAN *arrives with deck of cards.* HARRY *brushes him away. As* BARMAN *turns, he calls him back.* "Another round!" BARMAN *takes Harry's glass and the three others which haven't been touched.* HARRY *starts to protest, thinks it useless, drops his hand.*

THE ONE WITH PAPER BOATS (*languidly and without raising his head*) Yeah, whadda we waitin' for?

HARRY (*face brightening, moves his chair closer, leans forward on elbows, as if to confide something of importance*) Listen, you dopes. . . . (*Starts to chuckle.*) I just got a hot tip—

Voice drowned out by record, which has started of itself this time, and loud: "In the meantime let me tell you that I love you" Annoyed, HARRY *gives* HOODLUM *a nasty look, jerks his thumb backward toward jukebox.* HOODLUM *gets up, shakes the box; the record stops.* HARRY *meanwhile has resumed talk, but it's inaudible. He's laughing his usual laugh and slapping his thigh.*

HARRY (*now audibly*) . . . and I says—Sure I'm listenin'—whadduz it pay?

Music starts up again—same tune—only louder. HOODLUM *rises automatically, expressionless, but* HARRY *motions him to remain seated.*

HARRY (*to* BARMAN) Hey, Louis, take that goddam thing outa here, will ya?

MYNAH BIRD Do you mean it, dearie?

HARRY (*still to* BARMAN) Or disconnect it!

BARMAN *starts toward jukebox. Record suddenly stops of itself.*

HARRY (*to cronies, who look utterly disinterested*) Anyway, like I wuz sayin', it's all fixed. All we gotta do—

Music starts up again, of itself. This time it's Kate Smith—full blare: "God Bless America!" HARRY, *thoroughly enraged, dashes to the box, shakes it vigorously*

—enough to break it in pieces—and the music stops. As he starts back to the table, muttering a few curses under his breath, he collides with young GIRL *who has just entered. As she passes he gives her a healthy whack on the rump. The girl pretends to ignore it and goes straight to the bar, where she seats herself on a high stool.*

HARRY (*pointing finger in her direction and grinning at his companions*) Not bad, eh? Why don't you pick yourself somethin' like that for a change? (GIRL *sits with skirt well up over knee.*) Makes your mouth water, what? (*Gives his usual laugh.*)

HARRY *goes back to the table and downs his drink. The lights grow a little brighter at the bar.*

GIRL (*to* BARMAN) Who's that big mouth over there?

BARMAN Him? That's Harry. Don't you know Harry?

GIRL Seems like I've seen him somewhere. (*Glances in* HARRY'S *direction while lighting herself a cigarette.*) Sort of likes himself, doesn't he? (*Takes a good drag of cigarette.*) What does he do—besides blowing his horn?

BARMAN (*grinning*) I never heard of Harry doing anything, to tell you the truth. Lives on his reputation, I guess.

GIRL (*scornfully*) *Reputation?*

BARMAN Yeah. A football player—*once.*

HARRY *now looks toward the bar, gives a big grin meant for the* GIRL, *and impulsively rises, in his energetic*

*way knocking bottles and glasses over as he does so.
Walks bouncingly over to the* GIRL, *puts an arm around
her shoulder, and raises her dress—just a tiny bit higher
—like so. Meanwhile, the* HOODLUM *has gone to jukebox, dropped a coin. Music plays softly this time—
"These Foolish Things."*

HARRY (*looks at his pals while rubbing his hand over
girl's leg*) Classy, what!

MYNAH BIRD It's love alright. *Real love.*

GIRL (*removing* HARRY'S *hand from her leg and
dropping it*) Irresistible, aren't you? (*She gives a glassy
smile, then quickly changes face.*) Did anyone ever tell
you just how foolish you can look?

HARRY Sure, sure . . . but they like me just the same.
(*Puffs out his chest and grins.*)

GIRL (*jeeringly*) Can't help it, I suppose. Such a big,
handsome brute!

HARRY (*puffing chest some more and adjusting cravat
in pretended conceit*) It's the personality that counts.

GIRL (*laughing derisively*) *Personality?* (*Looks him
up and down. Takes time before continuing.*) To me
you're just a big hunk of flesh. (*Slight pause*) Sort of
cute, though, I must admit. (*Puts her hand on his arm
familiarly.*) Tell me, Big Boy, just what do you do? I
mean when you're not shooting off your mouth?

HARRY (*grinning, thinks he's making headway*) As
little as possible.

64

GIRL I know that. But what keeps you so fresh and healthy? (*More familiarly still, while pushing him slightly away to give him the once over again.*) Just a big hunk of flesh . . . And always in rut, I'll bet.

HARRY, *rather nonplussed, starts to give one of his horsey laughs, but breaks off suddenly, as if just getting drift of her remarks. Is about to protest, but the girl doesn't give him a chance.*

GIRL You don't know what I'm talking about, do you? (*To* BARMAN) Pour him a drink. . . . He looks like he needs one. (*To* HARRY) What'll it be—ginger ale?

HARRY (*flustered and looking slightly aggrieved*) Whadda ya trying to hand me? I'm not too bright maybe, but—

GIRL (*knowingly*) You're bright enough—when it comes to getting your end in. (*To* BARMAN) Wouldn't you say so, Louis?

MYNAH BIRD Pop goes the weasel!

BARMAN *serves drinks. Phone rings.* BARMAN *goes to telephone booth.* GIRL *and* HARRY *continue talking, but too low to be heard.* HARRY *has his hand on her leg.*

BARMAN (*returning from phone*) It's for you, Harry.

HARRY Who is it? A woman? (BARMAN *nods.*) Say I just left, will yuh?

BARMAN *goes back to phone. Returns in moment or two.*)

BARMAN No answer. She musta hung up.

HARRY If she calls again, you know what to say. (*To* GIRL) How come I never seen ya before?

GIRL (*lightly*) You don't get to the right places, I guess.

HARRY I get around alright.

GIRL Maybe you need glasses.

Phone rings again. BARMAN *goes to answer.*

HARRY (*to* BARMAN) Remember what I told ya!

GIRL and HARRY talk in low tones, heads close together.

BARMAN *returns, after longer lapse than before.*

BARMAN It's her again. Says she's *got* to speak to you. Sounds desperate.

HARRY (*irritated*) Cripes! I told ya to say I was gone, didn't I?

BARMAN I did, but she wouldn't listen. Sounds hysterical. Like she was gonna kill herself—or sumpin!

HARRY (*hesitating a moment*) Tell her I just left. Make sure she understands. Left for Philly, say.

BARMAN *shrugs shoulders and goes back to phone booth.*

HARRY (*taking a good slug*) She won't do herself in. That's just a line. I've had it pulled on me before.

GIRL (*raises glass, takes long sip*) I wouldn't be so sure, Big Boy.

HARRY (*quickly*) Whadda ya mean by that?

GIRL (*spelling the words out*) Maybe you're right. Maybe she won't kill herself. (*Slight pause*) But she might take it into her head to kill *you*. Did you ever think of *that*?

HARRY (*exploding with laughter*) *Her* kill *me*? That's the funniest thing I ever did hear.

GIRL Maybe it's not so funny either. Especially with someone like her.

HARRY (*quickly*) Whadda ya drivin' at? How do *you* know what she's like?

GIRL Maybe I know more than you think. (*She gives him a long look.*)

HARRY (*waving his hand as if to dismiss the idea*) Forget it! You know nuthin'. (*Takes a swallow.*) Listen, let's get back to where we started. (*Puts his arm around her shoulder.*) C'mon, tell me things. Where do ya keep yourself—and all that? Whadda ya do all day?

GIRL (*smiling mysteriously*) That's *my* business.

Music starts playing, softly—"He's My Man."

GIRL I'll give you three guesses.

HARRY (*quickly*) One is enough. . . . *Men.*

GIRL (*nodding*) Right! Now you know.

HARRY You're kinda young for that, aincha? Ya don't look more than eighteen . . . or nineteen.

GIRL Add another seven. I'm not a beginner, exactly. (*Looks at him teasingly, pretending to be seductive.*) To see me you have to pay. And you pay dear.

HARRY (*laughing it off*) *Pay?* You've got the wrong number, sister.

GIRL You think so?

MYNAH BIRD Take your time now. This way, please!

GIRL (*pushing him slightly away and sizing him up*) You know, you give me ideas. (*She gives him a significant look.*) Maybe you wouldn't need to pay. (*Slight pause*) It's just a thought. (*Puts a little more honey in her voice, as she leans over him.*) I could use a handsome brute like—

HARRY (*excitedly*) Not *me!* Don't look at me that way!

GIRL (*raising skirt a little higher, taking his hand and rubbing it over her leg*) I'm not so sure, Big Boy. You've got all the makings: no heart, no brains, no ambition. (*Provocatively*) Once you got a taste of me you wouldn't feel so squeamish. (*Raises her glass and drinks.*) Why don't you look me up sometime? I've got a cosy little place—not too far away. Plenty of food and drink—the best. And a nice soft bed. (*Slight pause*) I don't think the work would kill you either.

HARRY (*shaking his head*) I don't want any part of it. (*Pauses to reflect.*) Where did you say you lived?

GIRL I didn't say. *Remember?* (*She proceeds to fumble through her bag. Produces calling card. Slides it over to him.*)

68

HARRY (*scanning card*) Whew! That's right next door to—

GIRL To Jeanie, yes.

HARRY (*cagily*) So you know her?

GIRL I used to see a lot of her—but that was before you came on the scene.

HARRY (*sliding off his stool, as if to go*) I think I'll move along. (*Makes to go.*)

GIRL (*grasping his arm*) Wait a minute. What's the big hurry?

HARRY I'm getting restless.

GIRL (*signaling* BARMAN) One more . . . just a tiny one . . . before you go, yes? (HARRY *sort of gives in, sits halfway on stool.* GIRL *leans back, one elbow on bar, cigarette to lips, and coolly blows smoke in his face.*) You know (*as if it had just come to mind*), if it's Jeanie you're worried about, we could always find another pad.

BARMAN *serves drinks. They clink glasses and drink.*

HARRY (*playing along, feeling his way*) Uh huh! And while you're out hustlin' . . . (*jerks head to take words back*) . . . I mean, while you're out workin', what am I doin'?

GIRL (*as if the question were a silly one*) Taking it easy. What do you suppose?

HARRY (*mockingly*) I wouldn't have to hide in the closet?

69

GIRL (*ignoring remark*) You could go to the movies, see your friends . . . anything you like.

HARRY Uh huh. And when you got through . . . *with your work . . .?*

GIRL (*putting her hand over his*) Then it would be just you and me.

HARRY (*ironically*) You don't think you'd be too tired?

GIRL Not *too* tired. Not with a big handsome brute like you to play with. Besides, I don't wear myself to the bone.

BARMAN *now approaches and leans over the bar. He looks worried. Means to whisper in* HARRY'S *ear, but shouts instead.*

BARMAN She's coming, Harry. I just seen her turn the corner. Better beat it.

HARRY (*Makes for side door full speed. Stops halfway, returns to bar and pockets the calling card. To* BARMAN *as he goes out the door*) Thanks, Louis! (*Waves to* GIRL.) Tell her I went to Philly, ya hear? I'll call ya later. (*Exits.*)

GIRL (*derisively*) True blue, what! It's like I said—*all the qualities.*

Enter JEANIE, *bedraggled-looking, still clad in pajamas and worn bathrobe, hair a mess. Looks distraught. She enters very quietly. In center of room she stops, looks about. Seems unable to believe* HARRY'S *gone.*

GIRL Jeanie, what's up? What's got into you? (*She slips off her stool, advances a step or two, then stops.*)

70

JEANIE (*ignoring her, to* BARMAN) Where is he? Where did he go?

BARMAN Philadelphia. (*Turns to* BAR GIRL.) That's what he said, didn't he?

JEANIE When? How long ago?

BARMAN Just a few minutes ago. . . . Maybe a half hour.

JEANIE (*distressed*) You told him it was me?

BARMAN No. No, I didn't. He musta guessed it.

GIRL (*advancing toward* JEANIE, *who stands as if in a trance*) Come, sit down. He won't go very far.

JEANIE (*putting her hands over her face*) Oh no, no! (*Begins to sob.*)

The POOL PLAYERS *stare at her and move off. The men at the table get up and leave, one by one.*

GIRL (*taking* JEANIE'S *arm, to lead her to bar. Jeanie doesn't budge.*) Come, come, don't take it so hard. Believe me, they always come back.

JEANIE (*quietly and solemnly*) He'll never come back. I know it, I know it. (*She's about to weep again*).

The GIRL *now coaxes* JEANIE *to the bar. Orders something of the* BARMAN *in low voice.* JEANIE—*as if drugged —seats herself beside the* GIRL.

GIRL You mustn't take it so hard, Jeanie. He'll be back . . . I'm sure of it. (*Pause. As if to herself, but loud enough to be heard.*) If necessary I'll bring him back myself.

JEANIE (*electrified*) *You?* How? When? (*Her head and shoulders begin to quiver.*)

BARMAN, *who has fixed a sedative, leans over and hands it to* JEANIE.

GIRL (*taking the glass and holding it to* JEANIE'S *lips*) Here, take a good swallow. (JEANIE *takes a sip.*) Go on, finish it! You've got to pull yourself together. (*Pause. Pats* JEANIE'S *hand.*) I'll bring the bastard back on hands and knees.

JEANIE (*wiping eyes with sleeve, coughing, hiccuping*) No, no! I don't want that! *I love him.* I don't want anything to happen to him. He mustn't leave me, that's all. (*Slight pause*) *Not now.* (*She weeps silently.*)

GIRL (*putting her arm around* JEANIE'S *neck and bending closer*) What is it, Jeanie . . . did he get you in trouble?

JEANIE (*hastily*) It's not that. *I love him.* But he shouldn't have run away. (*She wrings her hands.*) He doesn't know what he's doing.

GIRL I know, I know. They're all the same. (*She strokes* JEANIE'S *head.*) Count on me, Jeanie. (*Her voice grows more caressing, more tender.*) Just leave it to me.

Lights dim, voice trails off; as curtain falls JEANIE *is heard sobbing.*

CURTAIN

Scene Four

SCENE FOUR

Few minutes later.

Street scene in tumble-down area of warehouses and factories. Street looks deserted, shutters down, except for a store on corner where streets intersect; in the show window manikins (undressed) in grotesque postures stand out conspicuously. The lamppost at corner is bent and the glass panes in the lamp are broken. The street signs hang assways and names of streets are illegible.

BLIND MAN *with cane enters from left, wearing shabby, very ragged overcoat; his poverty is exaggerated and he looks somewhat ridiculous. He walks gingerly and falteringly—tap, tap, tap—to center where streets intersect, directly opposite the empty-looking store with manikins in window. Wears big blue spectacles.*

HARRY *enters, running wildly. He is coming from round the corner (center). Collides with* BLIND MAN *and knocks him down.*

BLIND MAN (*in shrill, piercing voice*) Help, help! Police!

HARRY *helps him to his feet and hands him cane and glasses.* HARRY, *who is looking around to get his bearings, does not observe that as the* BLIND MAN *adjusts his specs a tiny light gleams first in one eye, then the*

75

other, then both together. (*Hardly perceptible*) *The*
BLIND MAN *seems to adjust his specs furtively.*

HARRY (*brushing* BLIND MAN's *coat hastily*) Shut up,
will ya? I couldn't help it. Why don't ya watch where yer
goin'? (*Realizing the man is blind*) Excuse me, I didn't
mean to knock ya down.

BLIND MAN (*in wailing voice, rather repulsive*) But
you can *see!*

HARRY (*more and more annoyed*) O.K., O.K. Pipe
down! I told you it wuz an accident. (*Looks up and
around.*) Where are we anyway? (*Looks up again,
notices dilapidated street sign—illegible—swinging
loosely. Gives the* BLIND MAN *a shake.*) Where are we,
you blinking idiot?

BLIND MAN (*in same shrill, wailing, quavering voice*)
I'm not an idiot. I'm blind, can't you see? A poor helpless . . .

HARRY (*putting his hand over man's mouth*) Where
are we, you bastard? (*Holds on to* BLIND MAN *with one
hand; looks around some more, rather frantically now.
Drops hand.*)

BLIND MAN (*raising his voice*) You're a thief. (*Yells.*)
Police!

HARRY (*again clapping his hand over man's mouth*)
Cut that or I'll give you one in the groin. I'm no thief.
(*Saying so, he slips a hand into the man's overcoat
pocket.*) Not a sound, *hear me?* (*Fumbles in the other
overcoat pocket.*) Where ya hidin' it? C'mon, I got no

time to waste. (*Now opens man's overcoat and starts going through his sack coat, then his vest pockets.*)

BLIND MAN *struggles weakly, gurgling and spluttering.*

HARRY Better fork it out—or I'll choke ya. (*In mollifying voice*) I don't want all of it. Just a few bucks.

BLIND MAN *begins moaning and squealing like a pig. HARRY shakes him like a terrier. Continues searching while glancing about in all directions. Finally digs up a few coins from man's vest pocket. Looks at them in disgust and flings them away. Desperate, he now shoves the BLIND MAN against the wall, his arm pressing the man's throat. He presses. The man makes a gurgling sound, as if choking, lets go of his cane and motions with one hand to try his back pocket. HARRY releases pressure but still keeps arm against man's throat. He fumbles under the coat for rear trouser pocket and extracts a wallet stuffed with bills. In his excitement he releases his arm from man's throat and proceeds to rifle the wallet. A few bills fall to the ground; he doesn't bother to pick them up. Meanwhile, the BLIND MAN slyly stoops for his cane and raises it to strike HARRY, who is still fumbling with the wallet. HARRY swings round suddenly, knocks the cane out of man's hand and gives him a poke in the jaw. The big blue specs tumble to ground, revealing in the man's eye sockets two square pieces of mica which gleam with reflected light. There are blue markings around the man's eyes, as if he had been the victim of an explosion. [All quite horripilating.] The man slowly sinks to the sidewalk, groaning and moaning as before. He sits with back against the wall, obliquely bent, like a stuffed doll.*

HARRY (*picking him up and dusting him off again*) Don't put on like that, you stinker! I didn't clout you so hard. (*Bends down and gathers the loose bills scattered around; he puts these in the man's fist and closes his fist for him. Gruffly*) Here, this'll hold you for a while. Next time you'll know better than to hold out on me. (*Bends down again to pick up the blue specs. Hands them to man. As the* BLIND MAN *adjusts his specs* HARRY *gives a shudder. He looks away a moment, as if it were too much for him; then helps the man to his feet. He grabs him by the arm.*)Look, I'm gonna walk away quiet like . . . and you're gonna stand right here. *Understand?* (*Sudden like*) *Where's yer tin cup?* Mind, not a peep outa ya! (*Brandishes his fist. The* BLIND MAN *begins to whimper.* HARRY *moves closer, menacingly.*) All that dough and pretendin' to be helpless. A bloody crook, that's what y'are. (*Moves off a bit.*) I oughta give ya another sock in the puss . . . fer givin' me all that trouble. (BLIND MAN *begins whimpering again.* HARRY *grabs his cane and makes a few faltering steps, in mock derision, tapping the cane and holding an imaginary cup in front of him. In a mocking, tremulous voice:* "Please help the blind! A few pennies for the blind!" *As he backs away he flings the cane to the* BLIND MAN, *who catches it with surprising adroitness.*) *You goddam skinflint!*

BLIND MAN (*recovering his voice, but not so loud now. Same repulsive wail.*) You're a thief. I knew you were. God will punish you yet.

HARRY (*Stops backing away, gives loud guffaw.*) Don't pull that on me, you dirty crook! *God,* huh! Ask God to give you a new pair of eyes. Yeah, try that! See where ya get.

HARRY *turns and walks slowly away toward the corner. He turns his head now and then.*

HARRY (*pausing a moment near corner*) Remember, don't squawk or I'll . . . (*He brandishes his fist.*)

As HARRY *saunters off, hands in pockets, he whistles softly. A man now appears in the show window, where the manikins are standing in grotesque postures, and deftly slips a tight-fitting one-piece bathing suit over one of the figures.* HARRY *pauses a second before turning the corner, then yells . . .*

HARRY: Go ahead now . . . yell yer fuckin' head off! (*Scrams.*)

BLIND MAN (*brandishing his cane and yelling at top of his voice*) Help, help! Murder! Police!

At the moment he begins yelling three old-time German street musicians with caps, short jackets, mufflers and bowler hats take their stand just in front of the window with the manikins and start playing in typical murderous fashion—"In Lauterbach hab' ich mein Strumpfer'l verlor'n. . . ."

CURTAIN

Scene Five

SCENE FIVE

A few weeks later: late evening.

The BAR GIRL'S *flat. Living room, with divan, dressing table and mirror, two or three low tables, several rows of shelves lined with books. Soft lights. Snug and cosy-looking. One door leads to kitchen, only partly visible. Center door rear leads to hall.*

HARRY (*slipping out of his jacket and kicking off his shoes*) Don't tell me you had a hard day again. (*Pours himself a whisky, with water from siphon. Stretches out full length on divan.*)

GIRL (*clad in filmy negligee, her back obliquely to audience, polishing her nails. Looks into mirror as she talks*) If I had, I wouldn't be telling you, would I?

HARRY (*stretching and waggling his toes. Extends one hand invitingly, as if to beckon her to come and be stroked.*) Ya can't say ya hear me complainin', can ya? (*Motions with one finger.*) C'mere, why don't ya? (GIRL *doesn't budge.*) That was a corkin' good meal ya fixed. *Mushrooms.* Who taught ya how to fix 'em like that? (*Pause*) Come to think of it, ya haven't told me a hell of a lot about yourself yet. What you did *before,* I mean. (*Points vaguely in direction of bookshelves.*) You musta been quite a reader—once. (*Lets his eye roam around the room.*) You know sumpin'? You got taste. Real taste.

(*Takes a sip.*) By the way, haven't seen Jeanie lately, have ya? Not that I'm worryin' about her. Just wonderin' . . .

GIRL (*still at her toilette*) You don't need to bother your head about Jeanie. She's . . .

HARRY You're sure she doesn't know . . . ?

GIRL (*hesitating a moment before replying*) Why? You're not afraid of her, are you?

HARRY (*sitting up*) *Afraid? Me afraid of her? (Tries to laugh but it doesn't work.)* Listen, you dropped sumpin' like that once before. Whatta ya gettin' at? Don't keep me guessin'! If she's got sumpin' up her sleeve, I wanna know.

GIRL *makes no answer. Instead, she gets up and moves about.* HARRY *looks at her as if patiently waiting for an answer, then settles back with a lazy, contented look on his face, as if he had dismissed the subject from his mind. Presently starts humming—"Sweet Sue." Suddenly sits straight up. Wears a blissful look.*

HARRY That's what I oughta call ya—*Sue. Sweet Sue.* Suits ya perfect. Always waitin' on me hand and foot. Think of everything, don't ya? (*Beckons again with one finger.*) *Come here!*

GIRL *doesn't move. Stands in center of room, regarding him thoughtfully.*

HARRY What's got inta ya? Ain't I been tellin' ya nice things? That meal . . . it wuz perfect! (*Snaps his fingers.*)

GIRL (*holding chin in hand, other hand on elbow. Looks pensive.*) Harry!

HARRY Yes?

GIRL What would you say if I took a job somewhere?

HARRY (*springs bolt-upright, electrified*) *What? A job?* Are you crazy? What's eatin' ya?

GIRL (*musing*) I've been thinking, that's what. Dreaming, maybe. (*Chuckles softly.*) Trying to imagine some other way of life . . .

HARRY (*quick as a trigger*) What's wrong with *this* life? (*Taps his forehead as if at a loss how to express his thoughts.*) Look, you don't work your ass off. Me neither. When ya want ya take a day off. No boss, no clock to punch. (*Slight pause*) Ya even get a little pleasure out of it. Or so you say. (*Grins.*) To make me jealous. I know. (*Pause*) Listen, don't get serious all of a sudden. It's bad for the health. (*Gives a quick look around.*) Not a bad setup. Let's make the most of it. You've got another ten years before ya show signs of wear. (*Slight pause*) As long as I'm around there's nuthin' to worry about. I take good care of ya, don't I? Haven't laid a hand on ya yet. Right? And I don't ask ya to work overtime neither.

GIRL (*as if she hadn't head a word he said*) I was thinking . . . maybe I'd like to be a manicurist. Or open a cosmetic shop.

HARRY (*wagging his head*) A cosmetic shop? *With what?* Whose money?

GIRL (*in same vein, as if talking to herself*) Or maybe an antique shop. I've always had a yen for old things.

HARRY (*roughly*) Cut it! C'mere! Sit down! (*He rises from the divan and starts walking up and down, first in front of her, then behind her.* GIRL *moves a few inches closer to the divan.*)

GIRL (*half talking to herself*) What I did before, you were asking. I was a salesgirl, a telephone operator, and for a while a librarian. Then I got the bug—about the stage. Thought I was another Greta Garbo. (*Takes notice now of* HARRY *circling about her.*) Sit down, won't you? I'd like to tell you a few things while I'm at it.

HARRY (*petulantly*) Sit down, sit down. . . . I don't wanna sit down. Ya get me jittery with all this drat . . . cosmetics, manicure, antiques. (*He goes to the divan; fixes two drinks; offers her one but she refuses it. Seats himself on divan with pained resignation.*)

GIRL (*feeling her way*) You know, Harry, you're not a bad sort . . . if one knows how to take you. But you're never going to get anywhere, that's for sure. Just the same, I like having you around. (*Pause*) I never mentioned it, did I, but you remind me of someone I was in love with once. (*Smiles weakly.*) I was pretty young. So was he. He was struggling to write. *Plays.* And I kept him . . . until . . . until he made a hit. That was the end. He ran off and married the star. (*Pause*) That's when I decided to work for myself . . . if you can call it work. (*Slight pause*) Yes, you have a lot in common. Only *he* wasn't the lazy sort. *He* wanted to get somewhere fast. And he did! (*Very low*) And I got lost in the shuffle.

HARRY (*sniffing the air*) What is it? Has he turned up again? Don't hold out on me! If you want *him*, just say the word.

GIRL (*scornfully*) Idiot! Why would I want him . . . now? Success was what he wanted, and he got it. As for me, I've been looking for love. Funny, eh!

HARRY What's wrong wid *me*? Don't I give ya plenty of love? Whadda ya mean, *love*?

GIRL (*shrugging her shoulders*) You wouldn't know, even if I spelled it out for you. The only difference between you and the suckers I take to bed is— (*Changes tack.*) One gets so damned sick of men. *Men, men, men.* No. I don't want you to clear out. I'd miss you. You're like part of the furniture.

HARRY (*peeved*) If it's that lovey-dovey stuff you're achin' fer, I can dish it out too. *If I have to.* With Jeanie it wuz different. She *had* to have it. It was like medicine.

GIRL (*resuming seat at dresser, but facing him now*) You don't need to do or be anything more than you are. When I'm sick of you I'll let you know. (*Slight pause*) Wouldn't you look cute now, bringing me flowers—or a box of chocolates? (*Pause*) Love . . . I'll tell you what I mean by love. When you love, it's the other person who counts most. . . . But don't break your skull figuring it out!

HARRY (*thumbing his chest*) You mean I only think about myself?

GIRL That's it. You and what *you* want.

HARRY And what about *you?* Who are *you* thinkin' of all the time? Mind ya, I'm not complainin'. But it aint love. There never was any talk about love between us. You made me a proposition, and I accepted. And I brought a little dough with me, didn't I? (*Gets up, goes toward her; stands square in front of her.*) What *is* all this, anyway? Whatta we arguin' about? (*He pauses, as if doing a real think.*) Listen, it's about time you had the curse, ain't it? Maybe that's what's wrong wid ya.

GIRL (*nodding head slowly*) Yes, Harry, maybe that's it. Maybe I'm starting a new period. . . .

HARRY (*quickly*) I don't like the way you say that.

GIRL (*half to herself*) I'd like to be looked at as if I were a human being. . . .

HARRY (*quickly*) You don't look like no tramp to *me* —if that's what ya mean. First time I laid eyes on ya I took ya for a kid just outa school. I didn't take ya for no whore.

GIRL (*flushing*) I'm *not* a whore! . . . Oh well, maybe I am too. Maybe I've always been one. . . . But I don't have to stay a whore, *do I?*

HARRY (*hesitatingly*) No-o-o. Not if you don't wanta. Ya can always wash dishes . . . or scrub floors . . . *or be a manicurist.* . . . That's almost the same.

HARRY *starts moving about restlessly.* GIRL *rises and goes to divan he has vacated.* HARRY *takes her place at the dressing table, knees crossed, toying with the nail file.* GIRL *sits back on divan, hands clasped behind her head. She looks quite relaxed. Wears a thin smile now.*

GIRL Let's drop that subject for a moment. I said I wanted to talk to you. (HARRY *springs to his feet at the mention of "talk."*) Sit down, why don't you? (*She looks at empty glasses beside her.*) I thought you fixed me a drink?

HARRY I forgot. I musta drunk yours too. (*Gets up, fixes her another drink, hands it to her, goes back to settee at dresser.*) Now then, what's on yer little mind? Spill it out! Don't worry about hurtin' my feelin's.

GIRL (*hesitating a moment or two, then coyly*) To begin with, supposing I told you I was in love? *Just supposing.*

HARRY (*giving a hollow sort of grin*) Go on, I'm all ears.

GIRL I hardly know where to begin. It's all so new to me. . . . Anyway, a couple of weeks ago, I guess it was, I ran into someone. He was just coming out of a movie. Very shy and very young. Didn't quite know how to tackle me. Acted like I was the first woman he ever tried to make. You know what I mean. *Romantic,* as you say. (*Pause. She clears her throat and sips her drink.*) The second time . . . I *think* it was the second time . . . he brings me flowers—and a poem. He said he wrote it just for me. (*Pause*) It's hard to explain . . .

(HARRY *sits very quiet now, like a cat watching a mouse.*)
All the stuff he spilled out . . . it was so wonderful to
hear . . . even if it came from the mouth of a kid. Maybe
just because he was a kid. (HARRY *doesn't bat an eye-
lash.*) It was all too good to be true. I tried to put him
off . . . tried to tell him I was just a bum, but it made
no impression on him. (*Pause*) Love at first sight, I
guess . . .

HARRY Go on, go on! Sounds cute like. (*Lights himself a cigarette.*)

GIRL Well, anyhow, that's what got me to thinking, I
suppose. It was the first time in ages anyone talked to me
like that. Of course, he's just a kid. But it's good to hear
the things you'd like to hear—even from a kid. I've felt
different ever since. (*Pause*) Anyway, what I started to
say is—the thought of taking a job appeals to me. He's
even offered to support me while I look for one. I don't
know *how*. (*Pause*) Poor kid, I feel sorry for him. What
have I to give *him?*

HARRY (*jeeringly*) You could be a mother to him. . . .
(*Begins to pace slowly up and down, glancing at himself
each time he passes the mirror.*) But don't let me inter-
rupt you. You were saying . . . (*He's holding himself in
but it's evident he's ready to explode.*)

GIRL I was saying it does me good just to hear him
talk. It's not always love he talks about either.

HARRY (*mockingly*) No? What then? *God,* I suppose. . . .

GIRL Not exactly. But you're pretty close.

HARRY I don't follow ya.

GIRL You probably never heard of it but . . .

HARRY (*expecting something different*) Go ahead, spring it!

GIRL Metaphysics.

HARRY (*jumping like a fish to the bait, eager to take the lead because he is fed up with her drivel*) That's where you're wrong, sister. *Metaphysics?* (*He cups one ear.*) Did I hear ya right? Listen, that's right up my alley.

GIRL (*open-mouthed*) Impossible! You must be thinking of—

HARRY (*at a gallop, like a horse with the bit in his mouth*) I know what I mean alright, alright. It's like homework to me. Want me to name a few? I can spill 'em out like beans. (*Makes a motion of pouring. Then, like lightning and with correct pronunciation of names, he reels off:*) Plato, Spinoza, Schopenhauer, Nietzsche, St. Thomas Aquinas, Duns Scotus, Roger Bacon, David Hume, Paracelsus, Bishop Berkeley (What a card!), Immanuel Kant (Cantilever Kant), Herbert Spencer, Descartes (a real jack-in-the-box, that one!). Is that enough for ya? I can reel 'em off backwards, if ya like. (*And he does. Pause*) Wait a sec! What about that fricadella . . . not Susa or Cusa—the other guy? I got it! (*Snaps his fingers.*) Pico della Mirandola! Try that on yer Wurlitzer sometime!

GIRL (*stupefied*) But Harry, how on earth?

HARRY Simple. I roomed with a guy once . . . a bit of a psycho. All he had on his mind was—metaphysics. We didn't either of us have much to do, ya see. (*He talks fast, as if to prevent her taking over. Also, he is fascinated by what's coming out of his own mouth.*) Now and then he'd read aloud to me. Not that I was itchin' to listen. I did it to make him feel good, that's all. He was a weirdie, just like I told ya. Of course, I never understood a word. It wuz just a big mess buzzin' around in my noodle. (*He taps his skull.*) But I never forgot the names. *Crazy,* what? Especially that Pico-what's-his-name. And *Erasmus.* Must be somethin' in a name, what? It wuz all a big jigsaw puzzle, like I said. But hypnotizin'. Always soundin' like it meant somethin'—but it never did. He might as well have been talkin' astrology. (*Brief pause*) Yeah, just when I thought we were gettin' somewhere I'd lose him. Like leaves droppin' into a sewer. No wonder he went nuts. Ya know, sometimes, when he got desperate . . . when he had to have an answer . . . he'd make me sit down and listen and then he'd say: "Now tell me what you think —*quicklike!*" Like askin' ya to talk about a record you heard a million times. "Say anything!" he'd say. "Whatever comes inta yer head." So I'd say sumpin'. *Anything.* Ya know what he'd say? He'd say: "*I think ya got sumpin' there.*" Rum, what? (*Pauses to blow smoke ring. Looks at it meditatively.*) Imagine . . . we work our ass off tryin' to keep alive . . . and these guys, these metaphysicos (*Blows another smoke ring.*) plant themselves in the clouds and spin cocoons. . . . (*Pause. Sits down again at dresser, facing her. Changes his tone.*) But comin' back to *your* problem . . .

GIRL I never got a chance to state it.

HARRY Well, I'm listenin'. . . . But don't dawdle over it, for Chrissake! You were tellin' about this Romeo of yours. Now what was it ya wanted to say?

GIRL Just that I'd like to invite him up here sometime. You wouldn't mind, would you?

HARRY Why should I? It's *your* place. (*Pause*) As long as he doesn't give ya wrong ideas. You're just weak enough to marry a chump like that. *Romance,* that's what you're after.

GIRL No, Harry. Not romance . . . *love.* Love and a bit of respect. If that means anything to you . . . Anyway, I'm not making any plans. I'm just wondering if it's possible . . . if it isn't too late . . . to lead another kind of life. There's no one I can confide in, except you. And you're not a great help. . . . I don't have any friends any more.

HARRY You got Jeanie.

GIRL I haven't seen Jeanie since we—

HARRY (*sort of relieved*) Not since we moved, ya mean?

GIRL (*nodding*) I didn't want to hurt her. Besides, I promised . . . (*She breaks off.*) By the way, haven't you ever thought of going back to Jeanie? She'd be a lot better for you than me, believe me. She could give you *love.*

HARRY (*disgusted*) *Love, shit!* You're talkin' rot. I wouldn't go back if she were to offer me a château and a Rolls Royce wrapped in cellophane. Why do ya keep harpin' on Jeanie all the time? I'm O.K. the way things are. And so are you, only you don't realize it. (*Slight pause. Ominous*) Listen, you're not goin' to open no cosmetic shop, take it from me. You're gonna go on just like ya have been—and I'm goin' to look after ya. As for that Romeo of yours, my advice is to give 'im the air. You can't take that love stuff any more . . . it'd ruin you. What you need is a vacation. You've been takin' things too serious. You need a change. To tell the truth, I could do with a change of venoo myself. (*Pause*) But get this straight—don't let that Romeo pop in here while I'm around. I'm not jealous . . . I'm just cautious.

GIRL (*startled*) Just what do you mean?

HARRY No tellin' *what* I mean. Keep him outa sight, that's all I'm sayin'. There's plenty of other places. . . . (*Drawing his words out*) *I refuse to be disturbed.* Is that clear?

GIRL (*slowly*) I see. All right, Harry, we'll arrange it some other way then. (*She rises and proceeds to get her clothes from the closet.*)

HARRY (*as she slips into her skirt*) Whadda ya doin'? Whatcha puttin' them things on fer? It's time to hit the hay. (GIRL *continues to dress. Finally slips into her top-coat. Never says a word all the while.*)

HARRY (*approaching her, putting hand on her arm*)

94

Whatcha up to? Where ya goin'? (*Gives her arm a shake*.)

GIRL (*pushing his hand away*) I'm going to see somebody.

HARRY Who? *Him?*

GIRL (*trying to get to the door,* HARRY *blocking her*) Yes, *him*. I want to warn him. . . .

HARRY Ya could phone, couldn't ya? What's the hurry, anyway? He's not comin' tonight. . . . *Or is he?*

GIRL How should *I* know? *He's in love,* I told you. And I don't want him to get hurt by a big, lazy bum like you.

HARRY So that's it? Jesus, I begin to believe you *are* in love. You're nuts. . . . And I'm a big, lazy bum, eh? (*He gives her a sound slap in the face*.)

GIRL (*recoiling, furious*) Don't ever do that again. I warn you.

Losing control of himself, HARRY *slaps her again, on both cheeks this time, and with the back of his hand.*

HARRY That's fer talkin' fresh. Now take those duds off and climb into bed!

GIRL *stands there, dazed.*

HARRY Did you hear me? Take 'em off . . . and be quick about it!

GIRL *stands motionless, pale with suppressed emotion.* HARRY *raises his hand to strike again.* GIRL *knees him*

95

and, as HARRY *doubles up, she pushes him away, runs to the door and out.* HARRY *slowly straightens up, groans a bit, ambles to the door, looks out, bangs door shut, flops on the divan, mumbling and muttering to himself. Silence for a few moments.*

HARRY That bitch! I'll fix her yet. . . . I'll fix him too.

CURTAIN

Scene Six

SCENE SIX

A few minutes later.

HARRY *is reclining on the divan; lights are low, gramophone is playing "Two Sleepy People" (Fats Waller). A drink is on the floor beside divan.* HARRY *keeps his hand on the glass while talking to himself in fits and starts. He is in a sort of twilight mood.*

HARRY She oughta be trottin' back soon, the bitch. A cosmetic shop, no less. And me behind the cash register, I s'pose. What a joke! (*Casting eye at bookshelves*) That's what comes from too much readin'. I shoulda burned the lot of them when we moved in. Can't be a good whore and read all that crap. Don't mix. (*Raises glass to take a gulp.*) Just a kid, eh? That could mean anything. He might be old enough to be her uncle, the little bitch. (*Stops to listen to the record; nods his head in time with the rhythm, hums a bit. Chuckles. Suddenly sits up, cocks his ear.*) What was that? (*Listens with ear cupped.*) Jesus, you'd think *I* was in love! What the hell would she knock fer? The hell with her! (*Sinks back.*) Let her stay as long as she likes. (*Pauses to do a little thinking.*) If ya ask me, they're not talkin' metaphysics. (*Mockingly*) You won't catch cold now, dearie? Make yerself nice and comfy! (*Normal tone*) Hey, wait a minute! Whatsa matter with me . . . ? What am I, anyway—a *morphodite?* (*Momentary silence. He lies back with a big warm smile on his face, enjoying his thoughts.*) Wouldn't mind if Jeanie were to pop in. She wuzn't such a bad piece, all in all.

The record stops and starts up again. Same tune. HARRY *gets up to turn it off. Halfway back to divan he stops. Thinks he hears a knock again. Stands looking at the door. A moment's silence. Now there is a knock, a timid one, followed by a second, stronger one.* HARRY *moves warily to the door, a knowing grin on his face.*

HARRY That's him, I'll bet . . . *Romeo.*

The door opens before he reaches it. JEANIE *is standing on the threshold, fully clothed, a handbag in her hand. She looks ravishing now. With a warm, friendly smile, she takes a short step over the threshold.* HARRY, *dumbfounded and sort of weak in the knees, retreats automatically, stumbles against the divan and falls back on it.*

JEANIE Hello, Harry! What's the matter? Seen a ghost?

HARRY (*stammering*) I . . . thought . . . it . . . was . . .

JEANIE You were expecting someone? (*She closes the door behind her, hardly turning to do so. Her hand lingers a moment on the knob. She advances slowly, seemingly in complete possession of herself.* HARRY *observes her in stupefaction.*) I thought you were expecting *me.*

HARRY (*goggle-eyed*) I . . . I . . . I was expecting a friend.

JEANIE (*mock sweet*) Not *our* friend, you don't mean? (*Slight pause*) You know, it was just as if you were calling me—long distance. Tell the truth now—weren't you hoping I would—

HARRY So it was *you* who knocked before? Eavesdroppin', eh. Who put the idea inta yer head? (*Slight pause*) Whadda ya want anyway? (*He grows more uneasy with each word.*) What brings ya here this time of night?

JEANIE (*with an almost angelic smile*) What difference does it make? I'm here. Aren't you glad to see me? (*Pause*) Don't stare at me that way! It's me, *Jeanie. Your* Jeanie. (*Slight pause*) Not such a bad piece either . . . all in all.

HARRY (*gruffly, but frightened and bewildered*) Whadda ya want here? There's nuthin' between us any more. (*At a loss for words*) Are ya tryin' to break up a home?

JEANIE (*unruffled*) A *home!* That's priceless. (*Takes a seat.*) Do you mind?

HARRY What's on yer mind? Don't keep me on tenterhooks!

JEANIE Don't look so worried. (*Takes an appraising look around the room.*) Nice and cosy, isn't it? (*She gives him a quick, penetrating look.*) With me around you'd have a bit of love too.

HARRY So that's it! She's cleared out, eh? And you're the . . . the substitute. Pretty clever, aincha?

JEANIE (*changing tone and moving to settee at dresser*) Not quite, Harry. (*She bends forward.*) All I know at present is— I've come to give you a chance. . . .

HARRY *A chance?* To do *what?* Take up with you again?

JEANIE (*measuring her words*) A chance to do the right thing . . .

HARRY (*quickly*) I told you for once and all—

JEANIE (*quickly*) Don't say it! *Wait!* Let me speak. . . . (*She continues as before, evenly, firmly.*) You never gave me a chance . . . not the least. You didn't care whether I killed myself or not, did you? You thought I'd get over it. (*Bends forward, hands on knees; regards him intently.*) Harry, if you had only five more minutes to live and you had the chance to say that you were sorry, that you still love me . . . just a little bit . . . would you do it . . . would you say it? I'm dead serious, Harry.

HARRY (*stutteringly*) What the . . . whadda ya . . . ?

JEANIE A lot depends on your answer. (*Slight pause*) It's life and death, Harry.

HARRY (*his mouth set as if to whistle*) Life and . . . ?

JEANIE Exactly. It's for you to decide.

With this she delves into her bag and extracts a gun. HARRY *springs to his feet.*

JEANIE (*leveling gun*) Sit down, Harry! And be careful what you do. Be still more careful what you *say!*

Don't try any tricks . . . it's too late for that. (*Pause*) Believe me, this is the last thing in the world I ever meant to do. In spite of everything I kept hoping . . . hoping you'd wake up one day and . . . Oh, I don't know what I hoped for exactly. (*Slight pause*) I never dreamed it would come to this. I don't want to do it, Harry, believe me. I'd rather kill myself. (*Dropping her voice*) I tried that too, but—

HARRY (*trying to cajole her*) Look, Jeanie, put that down a minute, will ya? You can't expect me to think with that thing staring me in the face. Besides, it might go off—accidentally. You wouldn't want to—?

JEANIE Don't worry, it'll go off when the time comes —or not at all. It's up to *you*. Take your time now—and think. Think straight . . . because it's your last chance.

HARRY (*imploringly*) But Jeanie—

JEANIE (*steadfastly*) All I want is the truth. I'll know by the way you say it. (*Slight pause*) I'd give anything to hear you say—I love you. But you'd have to mean it. The time for lies is over. (*Pause*) I've been through hell, Harry. I've killed you over and over—in my mind— but you always come back . . . you're always there. Like you were in the beginning. Believe me, it took more than courage for me to come here . . . and point this at you. To kill someone you love—out of love . . . it sounds crazy. Don't think I'm hysterical. I'm not. I'm not jealous, either. I've only got one thought—to find the man I lost.

103

HARRY (*hopes rising*) Jeanie!

JEANIE Yes?

HARRY For God's sake, put that thing down a sec. I can't think. I . . .

JEANIE I don't trust you, Harry. I'm weak, but I know better.

HARRY But Jeanie.

JEANIE Don't talk, Harry . . . *think!*

HARRY All I can think of is—when will it go off?

JEANIE It won't, if you think right.

HARRY (*gingerly, feeling his way*) I know I acted bad. . . .

JEANIE Careful, Harry! (*Points the gun more firmly.*)

HARRY (*bends over, head in hands. He is trying desperately to find an opening. After a time, softly, as if to himself*) How can I make her believe me? I'd get down on my knees and swear, if I . . .

JEANIE No need to do that. *I'll know.*

HARRY *continues to hold head in hands. Babbles to himself. Silence for a few moments. Suddenly a knock at the door. Startled out of his wits,* HARRY *jumps to his feet and makes as if to go to the door.* JEANIE *waves him back with the gun.* HARRY *retreats to the divan, lowering himself slowly. The door opens. A* YOUNG MAN *stands in the doorway. He looks at them as if he can't believe his eyes.*

YOUNG MAN Sorry! Must have the wrong—

HARRY (*excitedly, jumping to his feet, then quickly sitting down again*) No, no . . . you've got the right place alright.

YOUNG MAN I thought this was Miss What's-her-name's place.

HARRY It is, it is. Come on in! Miss What's-her-name will be here in a moment.

YOUNG MAN (*glancing in* JEANIE's *direction*) I think I'd better come back later. . . .

HARRY Not at all! Sit down . . . pour yourself a drink!

YOUNG MAN (*looking at* JEANIE, *but addressing* HARRY) You're sure *she* won't mind?

HARRY Tut tut! Of course not! (*He looks at* JEANIE, *then at the* YOUNG MAN). We were just havin' . . . (*Makes a vague gesture with hands.*) Well . . . how would you call it? . . . a sort of friendly chat.

YOUNG MAN (*ironically*) So I see. (*To relieve the tension*) A rehearsal, perhaps?

HARRY (*delighted*) Exactly. Ya took the words outa my mouth.

YOUNG MAN *continues to gaze at* JEANIE, *who sits motionless and expressionless, the gun still leveled. As if afraid to speak,* HARRY *motions to* YOUNG MAN *to pour himself a drink.* YOUNG MAN *does so, then sits near the door, always with an eye on* JEANIE. *After a gulp or two he tries to draw her out.*

YOUNG MAN (*to* JEANIE) I say, aren't you going to paralyze your arm that way? (*Points to gun.*) You ought to rest it now and then . . . don't you think? (JEANIE *doesn't respond.*) You know it *could* go off—accidentally.

HARRY That's just what I wuz tellin' her.

YOUNG MAN (*to* JEANIE) You could put it down a moment or two, couldn't you?

JEANIE (*in icy voice*) I *could*, yes . . . but I *won't*.

YOUNG MAN (*trying another tack*) If it's a play, may I ask who is the one who gets killed?

HARRY That's a good one. (*Pointing to gun, which is ever aimed at him*) Who do you think?

YOUNG MAN You never can tell—until the end. If it's a *good* play, that is.

HARRY You talk like you know sumpin'. You must be that Romeo Miss What's-her-name wuz tellin' me about.

YOUNG MAN (*embarrassed but pleased*) I don't know what she told you about me. (*He leans forward to hand* HARRY *a cigarette; lights it for him. Takes one himself, but doesn't light it.*) A drink? (*Looks to* JEANIE *to see if she objects.* JEANIE *remains impervious.*) By the way, if I were in your boots . . . what I mean is . . . if you were Rock Hudson—or let's say John Wayne—she wouldn't be holding that gun very long.

HARRY You don't mean John Wayne. You mean *Houdini*.

JEANIE (*to* YOUNG MAN) I wouldn't try putting ideas in his head, if I were you.

HARRY (*alarmed*) That's right. She's serious. This ain't no comedy . . . ya can see that, can't ya?

YOUNG MAN (*fishing for time*) I don't know what it is exactly, but it's not good theatre.

HARRY (*glumly*) *Theatre!* I wish to Christ it wuz.

YOUNG MAN (*fully aware of situation but still hoping to gain time*) There's one thing about scenes like this . . . they can be messy sometimes (*Turns to* JEANIE.) I mean if you don't hit the bull's-eye. (*Pause*) I take it you're a good shot?

Without a word, without a second's interval, JEANIE *shoots the cigarette out of the* YOUNG MAN'S *hand.*

JEANIE Does that answer your question?

The YOUNG MAN *looks thoroughly convinced.*

HARRY (*involuntarily putting his hand to his heart*) *Cripes!*

JEANIE (*to* YOUNG MAN) I think it would be healthier if you took a walk: I wouldn't want to make a mistake and kill *you*, would I now? (*She throws him a faint smile.*)

YOUNG MAN (*rising to his feet, but still sparring for time*) Do you think Miss What's-her-name will be coming soon?

HARRY (*eagerly*) Sure, sure. Any minute now. (*Turns*

to JEANIE, *half in earnest, half theatrical*) You couldn't wait just a little longer, could you? I'd sure like to see her before you touched that off.

JEANIE You're forgetting, aren't you, Harry dear? I told you you had a chance, remember?

HARRY (*eagerly*) That's right, so you did. I clean forgot.

YOUNG MAN (*to* JEANIE) If you'll permit, just one question . . . What sort of chance has he?

JEANIE *He knows. . . . (She levels gun at the* YOUNG MAN, *finger on the trigger.)* And now—*scram!*

YOUNG MAN *turns on his heel and walks to the door. As he reaches for the knob, he switches off the lights with the other hand. Instantly, two shots ring out. Complete darkness and sustained silence for half a minute.*

CURTAIN

Scene Seven

SCENE SEVEN

*A few moments—of eternity—later. Same setting.
The three are sitting in their usual places.* JEANIE'S *long
blonde hair hangs down over her shoulders. She looks
more beautiful than ever; her eyes are glittering. The
gun rests in her lap.*

*A few moments before curtain starts to rise we hear
Scriabin's "Fifth Piano Sonata" (a sonorous part); music
continues until curtain has fully risen. There follows
a full moment or two of silence. Then we hear distinctly
the sound of billiard balls clicking.*

HARRY, JEANIE, *and* YOUNG MAN *are looking at one
another in a rather dazed way.*

HARRY (*feeling himself all over*) What happened?

YOUNG MAN Whew!

JEANIE (*fully animated now*) I don't understand. I saw
you both (*she points*) lying there, *dead.*

HARRY When? Where?

JEANIE There! Right there! (*Points again to floor.*)

HARRY All I remember is the lights went out . . . and
me too. Like that! (*He snaps his fingers.*)

YOUNG MAN (*rubbing his forehead*) Seems to me *I*
switched off the lights. . . . *Or did I?*

JEANIE (*quickly*) And then the gun went off—*accidentally.*

YOUNG MAN And then what?

HARRY Yeah, then what?

JEANIE (*slowly*) I went to the door, switched on the lights, and there you were, the two of you, lying dead. *Right there.* (*She points again.* HARRY *and* YOUNG MAN *involuntarily look down at the floor, as if to see their bodies.*)

HARRY (*suddenly*) *The gun!* Where's the gun? (*Jumps to his feet and starts toward* JEANIE.)

JEANIE (*grabbing gun from her lap and leveling it*) It's right here, *see?*

HARRY (*raising his hand protestingly*) Not again, Jeanie . . . *please!*

Pause. Sound of billiard balls clicking—more distinctly. Sound comes from above.

HARRY (*cocking one ear and pointing upwards*) Listen! Where's that comin' from?

YOUNG MAN (*solemnly*) If we're not dead, then we're asleep and dreaming. I have a feeling we—

HARRY *is about to say something but stops with mouth open as music sounds again—from above. A few strains from "The Seven Joys of Mary" (John Jacob Niles).* HARRY, *visibly disturbed, grabs the whisky bottle from the table by the divan and pours. Downs it straight in one gulp.*

112

HARRY *Whisky* alright! (*To the* YOUNG MAN) Whadda ya talkin' about . . . *dead?* I know whisky when I taste it. (*Thumps his chest.*) You may be dead, but not *me!*

YOUNG MAN (*lugubriously*) Whisky is whisky, whether you're dead, alive, or dreaming.

Music changes to "Monotonous" (Eartha Kitt). Very loud.

HARRY (*stopping his ears*) Jesus, I can't hear myself think!

(*Music dies down; changes to "Sweet Sue," softly.*)

YOUNG MAN (*solemnly, as he looks heavenward*) I'm afraid the play's over.

JEANIE *meanwhile is sitting back in her seat, relaxed, listening to the two of them as if she had no part in it. The gun hangs limp in her hand; her elbow—of the gun arm—rests on her knee.*

HARRY (*sinking back onto the divan; less sure of himself now*) It beats *me*—if it's like you think. I pictured it diff'rent. Lights out . . . *wham* . . . blank. Instead . . . (*He raises his hand to indicate direction from which music is coming.*)

YOUNG MAN (*not so solemnly now*) Not at all. The lights may go out—but not *the* light. Soul, spirit, atman . . . whatever it be it lives on. It lives *through you, through me,* through all of us. The body is only a convenience, so to speak. So much baggage we carry around.

113

HARRY Seems to me I heard all this before . . . somewhere.

YOUNG MAN (*waxing poetical*) You heard it every time a bird sang, every time a flower opened. . . .

HARRY (*waving his hand*) I don't mean that crap.

YOUNG MAN Maybe you heard it in Sunday School.

HARRY The hell I did!

YOUNG MAN Or in your sleep.

HARRY *Or off Cape Hatteras!*

MYNAH BIRD'S VOICE *Wunderschön! Bitte, noch einmal!*

HARRY (*more startled than before*) *Hear that?* I thought we left that behind.

YOUNG MAN (*intrigued with his own words*) Only the Ghost has departed. We're in limbo now. Dead, but still in the flesh. (*He points to* HARRY *as if* HARRY *were an object.*) *That* . . . that body will soon fall away.

HARRY (*playing along*) Fall away? And what happens to *me?* Where do *I* come in?

YOUNG MAN You'll assume your heavenly body . . . the imperishable body, as we say. Now you're in your astral body . . . but you haven't accepted it yet. You're still carrying your earthly body around . . . *in your mind.*

HARRY (*ruminating*) Bodies, bodies . . . Seems I heard all this before. (*Slight pause*) Hey, wait a sec! (*Sud-*

114

denly remembers.) Yeah, it wuz that movie. The guy dies . . . but it's a mistake. It wuzn't in the book. So they send him back. (*Pause*) Lemme think! O yeah! In the meantime . . . between this place and the other . . . or vicey versy . . . I'm gettin' mixed up. . . . In the meantime his body . . . *this body* (*he touches himself*) gets lost or somethin'. There wuz a wreck, I think. Anyway, he has to wait around for someone to die . . . so he can move in. His body got burned up—or somethin'. You follow me? I remember that he's always changin' bodies . . . like ya change trains . . . but he can't change his personality. Get what I mean? Once (*he grins*) he slipped into a woman's body . . . by mistake. (*Bigger grin*) Wouldn't want that to happen to *me.* (*Pause*) Sounds *creepy, what?* Jesus, one body oughta be enough. . . .

As he is finishing his speech we hear the sound of a woman sobbing.

JEANIE (*in alarm and amazement*) Stop! That's *me!* That's *my voice!*

HARRY (*nodding gravely*) That means you're dead too.

YOUNG MAN Of course she is. We're all dead. How long will it take you to wake up to the fact?

Silence for a good moment or two. Then clear as a bell, John Jacob Niles singing "I Wonder as I Wander." HARRY *listens as music continues, visibly impressed. Meanwhile a door opens and an old woman, poorly dressed, shawl over her shoulders, market bag in hand,*

115

walks slowly through the room. Music continues. She wears a sad, worn expression. Looks at each in turn, but without seeing them.

HARRY Hey Mom! (*Starts to rise to his feet, then sinks back.*) Mom, it's me, *Harry.* (*Reaches hands out imploringly, while woman continues to other end and exits. Music continues to the end.*)

HARRY (to YOUNG MAN) I don't get it. She didn't even give me a tumble. (*Pause*) I never knew she was dead.

YOUNG MAN She isn't! That's why she didn't recognize you.

HARRY Whadda ya tryin' to say?

YOUNG MAN The dead can hear and see the living, but not vice versa. In the world of the living there is the real and the unreal. Here everything is real. . . .

HARRY (*waving his hand*) *Can it!* You're gettin' me confused.

MYNAH BIRD *C'est la vie, quoi!*

HARRY (*looking heavenward*) Cripes! Do we have to have that on our hands all the . . . ? (*Starts to laugh in spite of himself.*) It's gettin' to be a joke. (*Looks around as if—what next?*) Dead or not dead, I'm havin' a drink. (*He grabs the bottle.*) So what if it ain't real? Let's call it moonshine . . . what's the diff . . .?

As HARRY *downs his drink, the music starts up again, from above. The tune, done in slinky style, as on the old burlesque stage, is "Dreamy, Dreamy Chinatown . . .*

when the lights are low. . . ." All three listen as if en-chanted. Suddenly the door opens and the POOL PLAYERS, *followed by the* BARMAN, *all dressed like harlequins, march merrily through the room, with toy horns in their hands, singing:* "We are such fine musicians, we wander through the world. . . ."

HARRY (*pleased*) Never a dull moment. (*Shakes his head.*)

HARRY *has hardly finished speaking when they re-appear, this time dressed in convict uniforms, with stripes crosswise. They now carry trombones, which give the opening bars, then drop instruments and sing at top of their lungs while parading back and forth:* "Row, row, row . . . way up the river we will . . ." *fanfare and exeunt. All done in horsey style.*

HARRY (*spirits fully revived*) Ya know, I'm beginnin' to wonder. Maybe we're not— (*Breaks off, cocks ear, turns toward door. Listens with hand to ear.*) Was that a knock I heard? (*A moment's stillness.*)

HARRY *suddenly puts his hand to his chest, as if he had a pain. Sticks his hand inside his shirt. Pulls it out covered with blood.*

HARRY (*frantically*) Hey, look! (*Holds out bloody hand for* JEANIE *and* YOUNG MAN *to see.* JEANIE *rises quickly and rushes to his side.*) Look, I'm wounded. Call a doctor, quick! (*Sinks on divan.*)

YOUNG MAN Tush Tush! I told you you were dead. . . . A man can't go on living with a hole in his heart, can he?

117

HARRY (*frightened to death*) What? A hole? (*He looks down at his shirt where his heart should be. A big bloodstain now shows clearly over his heart. He opens his shirt and looks inside. Gives a low, drawn-out whistle.* JEANIE *now takes a good long look. The gun is still hanging in her hand.* HARRY *gets up, turns around, lifts his shirt high.*

HARRY (*to* YOUNG MAN) Take a look! See if there's a hole—where the bullet came out.

The music meanwhile is playing softly, "Illusion"— Hildegard Neff record.

YOUNG MAN (*going around* HARRY *and looking*) Righto! Clean as a whistle too.

JEANIE *also takes a good look, then slowly, thoughtfully, returns to her seat. Music now gives, but not too loud: "There's No Tomorrow"—Tony Martin record.*

HARRY (*to* YOUNG MAN) That's it. . . . I *must* be dead. (*Slight pause*) And you, what about *you?*

YOUNG MAN *turns his head for answer, revealing a small black hole in his temple, which no one had noticed before.*

JEANIE *now approaches to see for herself.*

YOUNG MAN Are you satisfied now?

Silence as all three regard one another.

Enter BLIND MAN *from left, dressed like an old-*

118

fashioned dandy, a boulevardier, with flower in button-hole, spats, gloves, and rakish light bowler hat. Seems young, virile, almost athletic now. Still wears big blue specs in which the lights blink on and off. After a few steps he resumes the faltering, shambling gait of earlier scene, but with exaggerated movements, as if made of rubber. As he walks to right exit, tapping cane, but more sprightly, he repeats: "Tap, tap, tap, down the weary lane" *in a cheery voice.*

HARRY I'll be jiggered! That's one number I didn't count on.

He has hardly finished speaking when the BLIND MAN *reappears, this time with cup in hand, and in thin, piping voice repeats:* "Help the blind! Please help the blind!"

HARRY (*irritated*) That bugger again! (*Springs to his feet and just as the* BLIND MAN *is exiting, he gives him a boot in the ass.*) That's what I meant to do before! (*Returns to the divan.*)

Music, very loud: Eartha Kitt's "Monotonous."

YOUNG MAN I say, it *is* getting a bit monotonous, what?

HARRY (*to himself*) So this is what it's like. (*To* YOUNG MAN) How long is it gonna go on like this?

YOUNG MAN It might go on forever . . . that's the trouble.

BLIND MAN *reappears, this time in full minstrel costume and make-up. He swings cane jauntily and twirls*

119

it. To the tune of "Suwannee River" he moves down front and center and executes a soft-shoe dance, à la Eddie Leonard.

HARRY (*laughing and wagging his head*) That takes the cake. Who'd have thunk it? It's almost worth dyin' to—

MYNAH BIRD'S VOICE (*in nasal tones of an old* clochard) *Sans blague!*

A momentary silence, followed by music of "Dancing Cheek to Cheek," from above. JEANIE claps her hands gleefully and rises to her feet as if to dance.

JEANIE More, more! I hope they keep it up! *Extends her arms as if inviting someone to dance. Executes a few steps alone. Stops suddenly as there comes a blast, extra powerful, from Edgar Varèse's "Ionization." The tat tat tat tat—tat part.*

All three look heavenward, as if hypnotized. Music stops and suddenly the door swings open. Enter HARRY'S *barroom chums, the* POOL PLAYERS, *the* BARMAN, *the* MIDGET, *all dressed in gorgeous silk costumes, like jockeys. They carry trumpets, trombones, cymbals, bass drums, clarinet. They march up and down the room and round about, acting like zanies, while blaring "I'm Just Wild about Harry!" They alternately play and sing.* JEANIE *dances by herself, her hair wild and loose, her blouse half open, seemingly delirious with joy. Even the serious* YOUNG MAN *is infected; he does a few fast steps on his own and yells a snatch of song now and then.* HARRY, *as if "sent," stands with mouth open in wide*

120

grin, and repeats insanely while pointing finger at his own chest: "Whadda ya know! It's for me, Harry!" *The musicians exit, only to reappear almost immediately, singing at top of lungs, "There'll Be a Hot Time in the Old Town Tonight!" They carry on even more crazily than before. As the turmoil dies down, and the musicians disappear,* HARRY *stands with hands on hips, watching them.* JEANIE *shouts:* "Grand! Just grand!" *With that the music starts up, above: "Dancing Cheek to Cheek." Impulsively,* HARRY *and* JEANIE *start toward each other, as if to dance.* JEANIE *is already dancing by herself, head wagging back and forth, in typical jazz-fiend manner.*

The music stops abruptly and now the BARMAN, *dressed like a comic German soldier, enters and moves down front center. With appropriate tin-soldier movements he sings "Hurrah for the German Fifth!"*

Note: If impossible to find words and music for this number, make it "Harrigan, That's Me!" with good Irish brogue.

HARRY (*mopping his brow and grabbing the bottle for another swig*) It's gettin' better and better, b'Jesus! What next, I wonder?

MYNAH BIRD'S VOICE Easy now! Easy does it!

A brief lull during which the three resume their seats. HARRY *sips his drink;* JEANIE, *twirling the gun on her forefinger, wears a beatific smile; the* YOUNG MAN, *hands folded, looks placid and resigned.*

Then from above, coming soft and clear as crystal,

an excellent soprano voice singing "Just a Kiss in the Dark." JEANIE *swings gently to and fro with the rhythm;* HARRY *hums to himself, appreciatively.*

HARRY (*musing*) That's one I always liked. (*Looks to* JEANIE) Eh, Jeanie? (JEANIE *nods, keeps swaying her head. Looks blissful.*)

Song has hardly died down when there is a blast from above, a military band playing "The Stars and Stripes Forever" (John Philip Sousa.) HARRY *springs to his feet, claps his hands over his ears, his face red with anger. Music softens, but continues.*

HARRY (*removing hands from ears and shouting at top of his voice*) No, no! Not that! Take it away! I'd rather burn. (*Waves his fist at imaginary Sousa above, while his lips move as if saying "Fuck you!"*) I did my bit, I did. Never again, not even if I'm dead. (*He moves about excitedly as he continues to rave.*) The Burma Road . . . that's where I got it. Had me scared shitless. (*Pauses brief moment. Imitates officer giving commands.*) Forward! (*He begins shooting imaginary gun— in all directions—like a man too frightened to know what he's doing.*) "Forward!" he says. The bloody bastard! As if it wuz play. Forward! And what does *he* do? Ask me! *Forward my ass!* I'm retreatin' . . . see? (*Moves backward a few steps.*) Don't catch me with my pants down. No sir! Not a second time! (*Music louder—a brief blast.* HARRY *sings mockingly: Da da da . . . da da da! Starts marching up and down with imaginary rifle on his shoulder. Raises gun to shoulder. Takes aim.*) Bang!

That for *you,* you bloody fool! Bang! And that for *you!*
Bang! And *you! (Drops gun to his side and turns first
to* JEANIE, *then to* YOUNG MAN.) Guess who I wuz
knockin' off! *(Looks down barrel of gun.)* I'm keepin'
one for the sergeant. *(Stops, thinks a moment.)* Yeah,
the sergeant. *(Flings gun away.)* I oughta *(he makes as
if strangling someone)* choke him to death, the bastard.
*(Bends over and picks up gun. Goes through the Manual
of Arms.)* Present, *arms!* Port, *arms!* Right shoulder,
arms! Left shoulder, *arms! (Drops the rifle. Comes to attention, clicks heels, salutes.)* Atten*tion! (Pause)* For-
*ward! (He starts moving forward, but gropingly, as if
blinded.)* And ya can't see a fuckin' thing ahead of ya.
Mines, torpedoes, flares, rockets, hand grenades . . . the
whole fuckin' works comin' straight at ya. Not even a
chance to wipe your ass. Forward, *shit! (Music gives
another blare. He looks up, shakes his fist.)* I hear ya,
you old futzer! Bad 'cess to ya! Ya hear that? *Bad 'cess
to ya!*

MYNAH BIRD's VOICE In the pig's arse!

HARRY *(pleased with the bird for once)* That's tellin'
him. *(Starts toward divan to resume seat. Reaches for
bottle. Pauses to reflect, still excited. Holds bottle, as if
intending to offer others a drink too.)* Never forget it.
The whole regiment wiped out. Like that! *(Makes
swiping motion with hand.)* Like so much hash. *Human
hash.* Chop suey. *(Raises bottle to lips and gulps.)* Join
the Marines, huh! Join the Marines and see the world
—shit! I seen it alright. I seen plenty. *(He starts to sit
down, suddenly changes his mind, and begins ranting*

123

again.) And don't ask me to take a job. I gotta job, *see.* I'm takin' care of this little gal here . . . and she's takin' care o' me. I'm an honest pimp, not a producer. And who are you takin' care of I'd like to know? *Nobody.* You can't even take care of yourselves. A-bombs, H-bombs, rockets, space ships, Venus, Jupiter . . . why don't yer just grab off another universe for yourselves and leave us in peace? I don't want your protection. I don't want any part of ya. All you do is louse things up. We don't want to grab off anything, you say. We just want everybody to be free, like us. The hell you say! We wanta gobble up the whole world . . . we wanta make the world over so that we won't have anything to worry about any more. Democracy, you call it. I call it cosmocracy. You don't want people to think for themselves, you just want 'em to think alike . . . like *you* think. That's what *you* call freedom. Not for me, brother. I'm diff'rent. I don't belong. I don't wanna belong. I wanna be a nobody, just an honest pimp, like I say. I don't make a stink about what I'm doin' . . . and I don't hurt nobody. I look after this little gal and she looks after me. Don't ask me to rescue the poor Hottentots . . . I got enough troubles of my own. I don't wanna kill anybody to save the world. It's not my problem. I got bigger problems. I got *personal* problems. Don't stuff me with a lot o' shit about other people's problems. I'm no Christer. I'm just tryin' to live my own life. And I'm doin' pretty good, except when you guys interfere. Clear out, I say. Take yourselves to Mars or Venus, any fuckin' place . . . but don't tell *me* where to go or what to do. I'm not takin' orders, do ya hear?

And stop wavin' that flag in front of me—it makes me see red. Red or dead, you say. Horse shit! I'm stayin' alive, whether red, yellow, green or purple. Nobody can make a bomb big enough to scare me. I've been scared already, and I'm stayin' scared—*of guys like you.* You're the enemy! You're fillin' us with hate and fear. You don't even promise us pie in the sky, b'Jesus! You want us to die because you can't wait to see what those bombs will do. You're so goddamned proud of your inventions that you're ready to blow us all up, yourselves as well. If that ain't crazy I don't know what is.

(*He sits down, his mood slowly changing. Lights himself a cigarette. He looks very serious, very sincere, as if moved to the depths. The* YOUNG MAN *has begun to hum softly "My Wild Irish Rose." Has a pleasant tenor voice. Seems to bring* HARRY *back to a good mood. Singing ends. Slight pause.*)

HARRY (*to* YOUNG MAN, *with quick glance toward* JEANIE) You know sumpin'? How do we know . . . ? I mean, how come *she* died? (*Looks to* JEANIE.) We never went into that, did we?

YOUNG MAN (*as if bored*) *Must* we?

From above, very very softly, like celestial music, comes strains of Ravel's "Introduction and Allegro," for harp.

HARRY (*rolling his head*) I'd kinda like to know. Wouldn't you Jeanie? (JEANIE *smiles but makes no reply.*)

HARRY *gets up impulsively and walks over to* JEANIE. *He bends over her and rests one hand on her shoulder. Speaks now with great sincerity, great earnestness. Like a new* HARRY. *Or the* real HARRY.

HARRY It's probably too late but . . . but I've been meaning to tell you for a long while now. . . .

JEANIE *looks up at him, eyes glistening.*

JEANIE Yes, Harry?

HARRY (*stroking her head, running his fingers through her hair*) I always loved your hair. (*Lifts her chin up.*) And your eyes. (*Slight pause*) I'm a no-good bastard . . . no gettin' away from it! But I never . . . 1 swear, Jeanie, I never meant to—

JEANIE *grasps his hands, looks up at him adoringly, trustingly.*)

JEANIE (*mumbling softly*) Oh Harry! It's alright, Harry.

HARRY (*caressing her head*) I didn't mean to run away . . . honest I didn't. I was scared, I guess.

JEANIE (*softly*) Harry, Harry . . .

HARRY You were too good, that's what. You never did a thing to hurt me. Never.

JEANIE *puts her hand over his mouth to stop him. He removes it gently.*

HARRY No, let me talk. I gotta get it out.

Music changes, softly, to "Comin' through the Rye."

126

HARRY Yeah, you were too good, too good. You were like an . . .

JEANIE (*brokenly*) Harry, don't! Don't say any more. . . .

HARRY (*looking into her eyes with deep sincerity*) What I'm tryin' to say, Jeanie . . . (*He takes her head in his two hands.*) What I want to say is—I love you. (*He bends over and kisses top of her head.*) Yes, Jeanie, I love you . . . I love you . . . I love you.

The music gradually grows stronger.

JEANIE I knew you did. I always knew it. Oh Harry, at last, at last! (*Slight pause*) Yes, Harry, I believe you. I always believed in you. . . . Now I'm at peace. Now we'll always be near one another, won't we? *Forever.*

She takes his hands in hers. They look at one another with eyes of love. Presently she begins to hum, and as the song comes to its end, she sings the words out in a clear, ringing tone: ". . . coming through the rye."

CURTAIN